PRAISE FOR *FLYOVER COUNTRY*

"In these fourteen hard-hitting-yet-redemptive stories, Luke Rolfes leads us into the Midwest we never knew, where storms pass equally across the plains as they do between fathers and sons, brothers, and men and women struggling to solve the mystery of their experience. Welcome to Flyover Country, a region extending from the Mississippi to your own secret heart. This is an extraordinary collection."

—Anthony Varallo, author of *Think of Me and I'll Know*

"Be warned, these stories will stay with you. It's a dark country in which people are at the very edge of holding on, and then they're over the edge and we're over the edge with them. Luke Rolfes, in *Flyover Country*, has done a very rare thing, he's given us lives of Miller Lite and TV, cut horses and gun shots in the woods, and done so with an elegance of description that both heightens their inherent hopelessness with a kind of beauty. These people we come to know scatter through our lives like the rain that comes down 'hard enough to stir the coins on the bottom of the river.' These are not easy stories. They're valuable."

—John Gallaher, author of *In a Landscape*

"Luke Rolfes is a natural storyteller who writes with a poet's love of language. In these perfect stories, he shows the extraordinary complexity of ordinary suffering. He shows the narrow margin between despair and hope. He shows that the Midwest landscape has a fierce and unique beauty--and so do its people. Those of us who live here are in his debt."

—Diana Joseph, author of *I'm Sorry You Feel That Way*

"Luke Rolfes' collection renders a mesmerizing terrain of humanity that 'closes down, contracts, and refocuses as something more precise like a photograph rendered at smaller resolution.' *Flyover Country* is 'the size of thunder' and 'the simple cadence of raindrops,' visceral and unforgettable. I am a huge fan of Rolfes' work. Get a copy!"

—Meg Tuite, author of *Bound By Blue*

"What the stories in *Flyover Country* are about deserve capital letters: Tornados, Baseball, Horses, Water, Sex, Paradoxical Desire, Family, Brotherhood, Love. That's why I like this book so much; it's about big stuff, the people and things we keep around because we don't know how to live without them."

—Richard Sonnenmoser, author of *Science-Magic School*

"The pain is quiet and the longing strong in these fourteen stories from one of today's most attentive, tender, engrossing writers of the American Midwest. Rolfes seems to know just how hard these men and women will be pressed before they give, and he seems to have a dead-eye intuition about the distinguished ways they will give themselves over to being pressed — pressed by the constraints of their families, their lusts, their formidable sense of determination and hope. 'Flyover Country' is a name given to a concept Rolfes' *Flyover Country* roundly rejects: you cannot fly over these stories. They are too absorbing, too urgent, too big and strong. They will pluck you by the scruff, as one of Rolfes' narrators would say it, and make you glad they did."

—Christopher Merkner, author of *The Rise & Fall of the Scandamerican Domestic*

"This gathering of fourteen short fictions is worthy of any serious reader's attention. Luke Rolfes's stories are varied and compelling. His voices are immediate and intimate. His subjects, troubled and tenuous human relationships, some of which fail and some which reach reconciliation. are profound. And he has a marvelous knack for the telling detail that makes a given milieu a felt presence. His rendering of nature, especially weather, never fails to create a vivid context for his narrtives. He makes a reader feel as if he knows as much about baseball, duckhunting, or the dangers of the ghetto, for instance, as the author. His characters are most often marginalized people, but their humanity is never less than tangible."

—Gordon Weaver, author of *Last Stands: Stories*

"*Flyover Country*, Rolfes' collection of smart stories, 'The Pitcher' among the best, creep up on the private cries and futile desires of people. Rolfes' insight illuminates his characters' fear of change, their desperate hold on the familiar, and their courageous, recurrent tries at loving and living."

—Nicole Helget, author of *Stillwater*

"The stories in this collection prove that this landscape is no mere "flyover country," despite the perfectly squared off sections that one might view from thirty thousand feet. It is a landscape that is, in many ways, more complex than that of the coasts—its subtleties thoughtfully limned by the author, an Iowa native, who, while extremely faithful to the landscape, is even more so to its inhabitants."

—Roger Sheffer, author of *Music of the Inner Lakes*

"The characters in Luke Rolfes' Flyover Country are tough. Early on in the book, one utters the line 'I'm not made of glass,' and this statement reverberates through the stories. The result is a collection detailing the real moments of fear, desire, and hopefulness that characterize many citizens in the 'flyover states.' Whether it's the loss of a house to a tornado, watching a brother enter county jail, or struggling to find purpose during a friend's wedding, Rolfes' characters stumble, fall, pick themselves up, and ask for more. They aren't treated like glass, and through the twists and turns of the stories, the reader sees a talented writer prove that the lives of these characters – like the lives of the real people in America's 'flyover country' – are vital and distinctive. Sharply drawn and richly detailed, Rolfes' Flyover Country will leave readers thinking about the people below the next time they look out an airplane window and wonder."

—Bronson Lemer, author of *The Last Deployment: How a Gay, Hammer-Swinging Twentysomething Survived a Year in Iraq*

FLYOVER COUNTRY

A COLLECTION OF STORIES

BY LUKE ROLFES

Flyover Country
© 2014 by Luke Rolfes

Books published by Georgetown Review Press are available at special discounts for bulk purchases in the United States by corporations, institutions, and other organizations. For more information, please contact the press at the address listed above.

Book design and cover photos by Stephen Gullette

First Edition

ISBN-13: 978-0-692-27787-4

Georgetown Review Press
400 East College Street
Box 227
Georgetown, KY 40324

http://georgetownreview.georgetowncollege.edu

Table of Contents

Acknowledgements

My thanks to the following journals for originally publishing these stories: "The Fish on the Lake's Floor," in *Bat City Review*, "Snow Geese" in *North American Review* as "White Sky Rats," "Ghostwater" in *Scissors&Spackle*, "Bugs" in *Permafrost*, "Honeybears" in *Connecticut Review*, "Shells" in *Iron Horse Review*, "The Tenth Highest Mountain in the World" in *Blue Mesa Review*, "Straw Man" in *The Baltimore Review*, "Mountain Passing" in *Passages North*, "Three Months" in *Georgetown Review*, and "Billy Ship" in *The MacGuffin* as "Horse."

I would like to express my gratitude to Steven Carter and the editors at Georgetown Review Press. I also need to thank the four people who breathed life into this book: Roger Sheffer, Richard Sonnenmoser, Ande Davis, and Diana Joseph. Thank you to these fine folks for helping along the way: Richard Robbins, Dick Terrill, Candace Black, Terry Davis, the late Roger Kirschbaum, Richard Black, John Gallaher, Toni Kay Cole, Matt Vercant, David Clisbee, Alyssa Striplin, Steve Pett, Danielle Starkey, Dodie Miller, Gary Roberts, Nic Dayton, my wonderful colleagues at Northwest Missouri State University, and my too-many-to-name friends in the MFA program at Minnesota State University, Mankato. Thanks to my brother Nate, Mom, and Dad for your love and encouragement. Thanks to Isaac and Jack for teaching me something new every day, and, most especially, thank you to Valerie -- my best friend, life's love, and center of gravity – who will never let me give up.

TORNADO

One of my brother Sidney's favorite activities as a child was to sit on the covered porch of our duplex with an elderly couple during thunderstorms. He didn't realize it at the time, but the retired couple was so poor they couldn't afford a television—even a black and white, but they loved how lightning cut needles through the sky. They loved the simple cadence of raindrops on the porch roof, the size of thunder. "It's big," the old man used to say. "See how it stretches from one end of the horizon to the next."

"All I see is lightning," said six-year-old Sidney.

"You could see it if you didn't watch so much TV," the old man said.

I ask if the old lady liked to knit. Why else would she describe lightning as a needle? Sidney can't remember. He was very young. This all happened before I was born.

My brother stirs cream into his coffee. It's early in the AM, and the Starbucks is mostly empty. A few people sit in the back, their faces bent over laptop keys or newspapers. The milk spins in Sidney's cup, turning black to auburn. You really want to know about the tornado, he asks me. If I tell you about it, I can't take it back.

There's an iPhone video on YouTube that shows a woman in a car lifted by wind. The phone, dropped between the seats, keeps filming. She screams the whole time. When the tornado sets her down, she shakes uncontrollably. Sidney thinks I should watch that video. That video would give me good perspective. These people always want their tornado to be an EF-5, he says. They want to survive the big one. It doesn't matter, though. The mammoth tornado that flattens a town full of strangers isn't nearly as scary as the little one that takes your house.

My experience: Sidney the dumbshit. If he hears the wail of a tornado siren, he doesn't go to the basement. He peers off the deck, contemplates climbing on the roof. He fishtails through gravel roads in his Toyota Corolla, eyes glued to the windshield.

I've always been afraid. As a child, I found tornado sirens unnerving. We learned in school that sirens were first used in London during the Blitz air raids. Seventy years later, the message hasn't changed. *Batten down the hatches. Here comes the monster.* The accompanying radio alert did little to settle my young nerves. Classic rock or sports commentary would stop, and then three piercing bursts of static. "From the national weather service in Kansas City," the metallic voice would say. "A tornado warning has been issued for Platte County. At 7:45 central time, the National Doppler Radar indicated a possible tornado touchdown east of Leavenworth, Kansas. Areas impacted include Weston, Platte City, Smithville. Residents of these areas should seek cover immediately."

Two weeks ago, the cottonwood tree in Sidney's front yard dropped several dead limbs. He wasn't listening to the television or radio. Instead, he stood outside breaking the fallen branches into sticks, stacking them in a pile on his empty flower bed. He remembers stillness in the air, a white sheet of clouds to the northeast, but the rest of the sky darkened to black granite and ash. You could taste the rain, he says, it just wasn't falling. High above, lightning flashed, but the clouds seemed to swallow the thunder. They went up and up, he says, as high as forever.

If he had concentrated, he's sure he would have felt the temperature drop ten to fifteen degrees, the coolness of the downdraft, an increased turbulence and electricity in the atmosphere. He might have even noticed the low, flexing wall cloud as it bore down on the neighborhood, the telltale rotation—a lit, spiral fuse. He doesn't remember any of the technical details.

He does remember a giant rush of sound and wind, and then the sight of a funnel-shaped cloud sinking in the bean fields to the southwest. The dust on the ground reached skyward, and the two connected. There it was: a twister, a cyclone, a finger of God. He said the f-word maybe sixty times. He felt for his camera phone.

10

He didn't think the tornado was headed his way until a fat drop of water struck his shoulder. The rain began to fall, wet pellets, and then cats and dogs. It was impossible to see, he recalls. Imagine blackness coming toward you, growing bigger and bigger, a man-eating werewolf howling in your face. The world in front of you separates—darkness in the middle, reality on the edge. He understood, then, that he was directly in its path. The tornado was going to hit his house. He could hear sirens wailing in the background, the faraway sound of someone screaming. He couldn't move for fifteen seconds, maybe thirty. Warm liquid trickled down the leg of his jeans.

Jesus, Jesus, he said, and then ran to his front door, desperate for his keys. After fumbling through his pockets, he tumbled down the split foyer steps. Moments later he buried himself amongst boxes of old soccer equipment and sweatshirts in the crawlspace under the stairs. It was odd, he recalls, not seeing the thing that was coming to kill you.

Beneath the stairs was quiet at first, but then the pulsing started. A freight train makes a constant noise, but this sound had contractions, waves. Louder and louder. The walls throbbed with each beat, the windows shattered. When the staircase began to sway back and forth, Sidney closed his eyes. If that is how you die, he says, you can't hear yourself think. You can't even conjure up the last face you want to see.

Other people in Sidney's town didn't survive. He didn't know any of the eight people killed. Most of them lived in the prefabs on the west side of the city limits.

Sidney did lose a pair of oversized goldfish: Big Boy and Whopper. They, along with the majority of his house, were lifted four hundred feet into the sky. He likes to think the fishbowl landed in another town. Old tornado set her gently on a little kid's front lawn, or dumped the fish in Smithville Lake. More likely Big Boy and Whopper landed off Highway 92 in some field or gravel road. They probably flopped around a bit. They might have rolled into a puddle and survived, at least for a little while.

I try to imagine myself isolated, huddled in the crawlspace under the stairs, one hundred fifty mile-an-hour wind ripping everything I own out from under me. The roof goes first, pulled loose end to end like a Band-Aid. Then the living room set, the recliner, the TV, Big Boy and Whopper, the dishes and all the pots and pans and towels. The fridge, frozen hamburger, bottles of half full juice and milk, even the neglected, expired food. The walls, the carpet, the floorboards. Pictures. Memories. Thoughts. Up in the air. The tornado takes it all.

———

There's one photograph in particular I remember. Maybe it's the last face I would like to see before getting sucked into oblivion. Maybe it's meaningless. I can picture the photograph in my mind, spinning upward to the heavens: me as a little kid, buried in a pile of crisp leaves, gold and brown puzzle pieces. I look like a creature of sorts—a disembodied head floating in a sea of leaves, strands of branches in my hair, laughing, two teeth missing. In the photo, my mother reaches toward me. Her lean arms and strawberry hair are a touch darker than mine.

It's been fourteen years since our mother moved out, here one moment gone the next. I'd like to compare her departure to the way the tornado left Sidney huddled in the foundation of his home, but it wasn't like that at all. There was no cold recognition. We didn't understand ourselves as forever changed. No one knew she would simply disappear. I had just begun to experience life as a teen, so I didn't cry or throw a big fit or try to talk her into stay-ing. I told her I didn't care if she went. I thought it was true at the time. Part of me assumed she would be back in a few days, cook-ing pancakes and sausage links in the kitchen, promising to never leave our sides again. Sidney was twenty, entering his sophomore year at Northwest Missouri State, so he wasn't there to teach me how to react.

She sat me down, my mother, and said that she didn't love it anymore. I asked if she meant Dad, but she said that wasn't what she was talking about. Not exactly. I don't love all of it, she said. I don't love this house, this town, the land, the stupid river and its floods. I don't love the same conversations and faces. If you see something so many times, you simply can't look at it any longer. I don't know why I remember this, but she wore a yellow dress, and her hair was caught in a long ponytail—one of the few times I had seen her outside of jeans and a t-shirt. I asked where she was going. She took my wrist and held it in the air. She tried to make me smile. Feel that wind, she said. I'm going wherever it wants to take me.

She hugged me for a long time, and I let her. She didn't cry, not when she pulled away from my skinny arms, not when she backed her car out of the driveway. Maybe I hate her for that. The hard part, when you're fourteen, is to not think it's you. You're the thing she doesn't want to look at anymore.

If I could do it again, I would ask when she was coming back. That was important, especially when the answer was not in the next fourteen years. I'll be twice as old, and she still hasn't called, she still hasn't written. I might have told her how strong I would become in her absence, Sidney too—so strong that we don't even resent her. We would grow up without her and become men, men who fought tooth and nail to protect each other, and we would crash headlong into anything or anyone who tried to hurt us, even her. You'll never see how good we become without you, I might say. But when you're fourteen, you get distracted. You worry about trivialities like if you play basketball well enough to make first string, or what it tastes like to kiss a girl with your tongue. How will your skin ever feel comfortable enough to let a girl see you naked? Why did it feel so good when you ran six miles in the rain, that one time, and you came home and took a shower lying in the bathtub with your clothes on?

Sidney hasn't touched his coffee. He's looking past me through the window of the Starbucks. You can see it in his eyes. The next part is hard to say.

I thought it would never end, he says. He felt water dripping on the back of his neck, but he couldn't open his eyes. The house was gone. The walls, the bricks, everything. For all he knew, he might be dead.

When the rain stopped, he climbed out of the wreck into his

yard. At first, he didn't know what he was looking at, but there was a woman next to the trunk of the cottonwood tree. The body of a woman. The wind had left her there.

I tell him to stop. He doesn't have to finish the story.

He shakes his head. It's too late. He's already gone too far.

BILLY SHIP

The kid made it hard. His moppy hair. Goofy smile with no front teeth. The way he sat cross-legged on the carpet and played Transformers. Transformers were stronger than He-Man, he told me, but not as fast as G.I. Joe. Most Transformers exploded if you dunked them in water because they were machines, but his were special. He coated them in sealant, like the stuff you put on decks to stop rain getting up in the wood. He didn't call me dad or sir or mister like his mother asked. I would have adopted him for sure, if things had been different.

I was on the phone when his mom left me, packing up her stuff in the bedroom. The kid was standing in front of me with a worn pack of Uno, trying to get me to fall for the old pick-a-card-any-card trick. Over the phone, my friend Charlie was telling my one ear about this temp job he had lined up for me, real good pay but kind of strange. "Seven of clubs," I said.

The kid cracked up laughing. "No, you can't see the cards, you've got to pick one out," he said. "Here, take this one." He handed me a five.

Over the phone, Charlie asked what the hell I was talking about. I told him never mind. Whatever it was, I'd take it. I needed money real bad. They were going to repossess my car soon, and I couldn't stand to see it go. That car meant something. '76 Stingray. All muscle. About two years back, my grandpa drove out to the shop with me to see it. He circled the body, pressed against the paint with his hands, checked under the hood. He said he was impressed, but that was a lot of car for me to afford. I told him not to worry.

After Charlie gave me the info, I hung up. The kid was looking furiously through his stack of cards, making a big show of it like he couldn't find the right one. I was thinking about when we picked up the Stingray, how that was the last time I saw Grandpa outside, walking on his own. Now he sits in his chair at the nursing home.

"It's a three, isn't it?" the kid said. "Just like this one?"

"How did you know?" I said.

He started to explain, but Donna, the kid's mom, entered the hallway, struggling with a box. She told him to head to the car so she and I could say our goodbyes. He understood what that meant. I should have said something, anything, as he walked toward the door, given him a hug or a hundred dollar bill, even though I didn't have either one to give.

When Donna saw the kid out in the yard, kicking at the dandelions, the tears started to fall. I stepped forward, but she took a step back. The bills, the late nights, the yelling that took the place of kissing. She said she wished things had turned out different, but I understood, didn't I?

"Sure," I said. "You can't hurt me much."

———

It was a strange job, the one Charlie lined up. He called it a horse aide. It wasn't hard. Days I had to myself. Evenings I shoveled manure, ran feed, swept up. At night, I slept on a cot in a racehorse's pen—kept him company, so to speak. Apparently, a horse needs friends. Some horses enjoy a hound dog around at night. Some like a pony. Others want a goat. This particular horse couldn't sleep unless a person was there, real finicky like that. He had an odd name: Billy Ship. People always name horses something weird.

Now, I'm no expert, but this horse seemed special. Billy Ship looked fast. Dark brown with a white stripe down the middle of his face. Built like a tank. Muscles on top of muscles, even in his cheeks. Legs like pistons. You'll never believe this, the horse was sensitive. Yell at him, and his head goes to the ground. Feed him an apple, and he's your best friend. Nuzzles your hand like a cat that wants to be scratched. If I had a bigger cot, he would have climbed in bed with me. He was still a colt, two years old, but the owners said he could fly. Said he had the speed of Smarty Jones but a little more intensity. He could do the long sprints, too. Needs race, they said. Billy Ship got jacked up when there were other horses around. Not mean; more like arrogant. He wanted them to know he was the best. He'd prance up to the starting block, snort and stretch his neck, kick the dirt, show off his build. The trainer had to brush him one hundred times, shampoo his mane twice, or else Billy got irritated; he wouldn't race his best. The trainer called it insecurity. I called it vanity.

I didn't like sleeping next to Billy Ship. At least not right away. A horse is a full-sized beast, not comforting like a spaniel curled up by the front door. The first night I had trouble dozing off, and so did he. I wasn't certain what a horse was capable of. He could kick me in my sleep, jump up and stomp my face with his hooves. Even him sitting on me would probably make me give up the ghost. But Billy was afraid, and he hid in his corner until I fell asleep.

The first time I woke, he was standing above me, eyes open, looking down. More curious than anything. "Knock it off," I said and rolled over so he'd leave me alone.

I remember waking a second time, later that night, the sweet smell of manure and hay in my nose. Billy was standing still in the middle of the pen with his eyes closed, his ears flat, and his lips slack. The moonlight shone in through the window, catching his large outline. For a moment, he didn't seem alive at all. He was a horse sculpture in a museum, made of stone, clay, dirt, and sticks. He was a statue in the garden of castles, a ballroom tapestry, the scratching on a cave wall. He was the horse that generals rode into battle, plated with steel and spikes, spitting fire from the mouth. He was the stallion that chased fillies through the Rocky Mountains with wind in his eyes. He wasn't simply a horse. He was what all the other horses wanted to be. The strongest and the fastest.

The king of horses. I remember thinking, what kind of fence could hold this animal?

The third time I woke he was sprawled on the ground, his belly moving up and down.

———

The next day my grandpa laid into me at the home. He said I should never have let Donna go. Wasn't acting the part of a man. That I hung out with Charlie too much, played too much poker for money. Didn't spend enough time doing important things like looking for steady work, making Donna feel like a princess, taking the kid out for ice cream. I spent too much time in the old folks' home. That wasn't any place for a young man.

"They take that Stingray from you, yet?" he wanted to know.

"They aren't getting it," I said. "I'm working again."

"Yeah?"

I shrugged. Better not to talk about it. That would lead to another lecture. Sleeping next to a horse wasn't a real job. At least not to a man who worked aluminum for thirty-five years. Imagine the hottest place on earth, he used to say, then add ten degrees. They wore suits lined with ice packs to keep from fainting. Most men were afraid of the height that Grandpa climbed to his crane each morning. Very few put in a full tour of duty. Fewer still made their entire pension. He was still tough, too, even for an old guy. He'd crush your hand in a shake. Wore shirts a size too small, but he was more gut now than pecs and biceps.

"Your color looks good," I said, changing the subject. "Do you feel like going outside today?"

"Feel like I should take a bottle of pills and whiskey. Get this over with," he said.

"Don't talk that way when I'm here."

He snorted and crossed his arms. I had this picture in my mind of Gramps as a young man—full of piss and blood. You could tell he had been scrappy, used to wrestle competitively before it was a sport. He always said to jack a man right in the chin if given enough attitude. Fight dirty, win at all costs. He was the type of guy who wore a flat-top, white v-necks, and blue jeans every day. Maybe even a pack of smokes up his sleeve. Drove a '65 Mustang hard. Spent a night or two in the clink. Let girls chase him, not the other way around. I imagined he liked Johnny Cash, but I don't know for sure.

He still carried a blue bandanna in his pants pocket. Had since my age. That bandanna got some use. Sometimes it mopped the sweat from his face. Sometimes it eased the pressure of a sharp object against his palm. A time or two it cleaned mud off a pock-etknife, wiped oil from a dipstick, and, more than once, it held a grandson's skinned knee or stopped a bloody nose. I only saw him put it to his eyes once, and that was when Grandma passed. It wasn't very long, either—just a second or two in the cemetery, when they started to shovel the dirt. Those tears never made his cheeks. The bandanna got them first.

I wondered if we'd have been friends, me and Gramps, had we grown up at the same time. I hoped he would have invited me for a beer, a shot of Wild Turkey, a burger and fries. I'd like that. He might have let me crawl under the hood of his '65, and he would have pointed out the things he was going to change: the hoses that had to go, the parts that needed a wrench pull here and there, the shine of the pistons and the carburetor. He'd tell me he kept it all damn clean, like you were supposed to. And he never raced it too hard. That was how you hurt a car, he'd say. Maybe he'd call me up when he ran the '65 off the road in an ice storm, close to tears, and he'd ask if I'd come over and be with him. He'd ask if I'd help him salvage what was left.

Or maybe we would've driven around. Him at the wheel, me at shotgun. The radio loud, sunglasses on, the roads straight and flat. I thought about taking him for a drive, then, in the Stingray I wouldn't let my creditors take. I thought about driving him across town to meet Billy Ship, and he could run his fingertips over that horse's powerful back.

Grandpa shifted in the wheelchair. One hand slipped off his lap and dangled next to the spokes. It had been holding the blue bandanna. The bandanna fell between his legs, crumpled, like a wadded piece of tissue. It looked worn out. Like it didn't serve a purpose anymore—something inanimate—something he just kept around because he didn't know how to live without it.

When I looked at the bandanna, I got a funny feeling in my stomach, as if I knew with absolute certainty that Grandpa was going to die soon. Not right away. He wasn't on his deathbed. But he would never make it to next spring.

"I'm going to get Donna back," I said. "She just needs time."

Grandpa wasn't listening. His chin had fallen to his chest. His shoulders bobbed, and when I leaned closer, I could hear him snoring softly. He looked like the rest of them—faces down, backs slumped, waiting for their breath to stop. I grabbed my jacket and headed to the door. That wasn't him. He wasn't like them.

———

A month or two later, Grandpa did see Billy Ship. The horse had started to generate buzz, so I took him and the kid to the track on a Sunday afternoon. That horse couldn't lose. Incendiary is what the boss called him. You could see it when he trained. Billy had fire in his legs. He knew when he won, too. Each night leading up to a race he'd toss and snort and stare at me into the early hours of the morning. After a race he slept like a corpse. If not for his heaving belly, I would have called the vet.

I put a twenty down on Billy; he was going off two to one. I figured that was an easy way to double up. I should have bet my entire check. The kid wanted to push Grandpa's chair, and I let him. I ordered popcorn and a couple of Cokes.

"When's the fast horse gonna run?" the kid kept saying. "Mr. Billy Ship."

"In a bit," I said. "Stop asking."

I felt completely happy, to tell the truth. Me, Grandpa, and the kid. A regular boys' night out. If there was a point in life I could go back to, it was that hour when we sat in the bleachers, our feet kicked up on the guardrail, sipping Cokes and watching the races. It became easy to imagine that Donna and I were married, the kid was mine, and it was son, dad, and great-grandpa sitting in the fading light of the afternoon. The sky stretched pink over our heads. The air was warm. We sat comfortable in t-shirts and jeans. The kid had a stuffed nose, and he snuffled after each bite of popcorn. When I bent my head down to hear his questions, his breath smelled like salt and butter, but I didn't mind. He could have dumped his Coke in my lap, and I would have run to get him another.

Two races before Billy's, a man named Andrews yelled the f-word a couple of times when his horse started to lose. He was sitting in the row behind us. I asked if he'd watch his mouth in front of the kid.

"Sure," he said. "I'm the asshole who left his son at home."

"We're just here to watch the horses," I said.

"You taking him to the tit bar next?"

I would have let it drop, but Grandpa chimed in. "He asked you to mind your language," he said. Ten years ago he'd have slugged the guy. Gotten us all thrown out. He looked at me, red-faced, as if he wanted me to do it for him. No way would he let it drop. I felt sweat on my palms as I sensed Grandpa sizing me up, trying to figure out what kind of man I was, what I was made of. Would I let a drunk ruin our night, or would I do something about it? I did the first thing that popped into my head.

"Be right back," I told the kid.

I motioned for the man to follow me to the betting window. He was wearing a dress shirt, slacks, and no tie. A big man. Straight black hair, caught in a pony tail, big arms and a big mustache. Probably part Mexican or Italian. I had seen him before at Charlie's poker games. He had played college football at Tennessee one year, but got cut because of grades. Charlie said he was the type of guy you folded a hand to if too many chips were on the table. His breath smelled of booze, but he walked straight. I knew if he hit me, I'd have to hit back. I'd never win a fight against a man that big, even a drunk. I held up a hand when we stepped out of the

21

bleachers.

"Andrews, right?" I said. "Friend of Charlie's?"

The man unbuttoned his shirt cuffs, rolled his sleeves.

"I'm not going to fight you," I said.

"The hell you aren't."

"How much did you lose?" I said.

He shook his head. "Not buying your way out of this."

"I'm not trying to buy anything. I'm trying to make you money."

"Enough talk."

"Bet it back," I said. "Whatever you lost. Bet it back. I know a sure thing. Pays two to one."

"You tryin to tell me this a fixed race?"

"Ain't no *race*," I said. "Ain't no competition. Not to this horse. "

He jabbed his finger into my chest. "I know you," he said. "You went to school with Charlie. Brought a case of Coors Light last weekend. I don't trust a guy who brings Coors Light to a card game."

I looked toward the bleachers. I imagined the kid asking Grandpa where did I go, and Grandpa saying I went to get a hotdog. I should have kept my mouth shut; should have let this man say whatever he wanted. It didn't matter. The kid wasn't mine. What did I care? There wasn't any way back to the bleachers now. I couldn't get out of this without a fight, and I couldn't have a fight and not get thrown out. I reached for my wallet.

"300 bucks," I said. "Bet whatever you lost plus my 300. Split the winnings."

I wish I hadn't done it. Given Andrews the money. No reason behind it. I didn't know him. He could have pocketed the cash on his way out the door, but I wasn't thinking about that. I wanted to get back to those bleachers. Back to Grandpa and the kid.

Andrews gave me a strange look but took the money.

"If you're lying to me," he said, "now's the wrong time to do it."

When I sat back in my seat, things started to sink in.

"Get it all sorted out?" Grandpa asked.

"Yeah," I said. "Everything's okay."

But everything was not okay. If Billy lost, I had gotten myself into worse than a fight. Much more was at stake. Not just my pay-check, but Grandpa's respect, seeing the kid, driving my car. I'd never bet that much before.

I saw Andrews standing in line talking on his cell phone. He gave me a thumbs up. I didn't realize it at the time, but he was betting a lot more money than he lost. A whole lot more. More money than I made in six months. Little did I know that it wasn't just my paycheck and my pride on the line. Charlie told me later that if Billy had lost, I probably wouldn't have woken up the next morning. This guy or one of his friends would have taken me for a walk. Stuck me with a knife or shot me between the shoulders. Rolled me into the ditch. I shudder each time I think about it. The night Billy Ship's legs saved my life.

I couldn't talk during the race, even though Billy led by three lengths the whole way. The jockey never swatted him. He broke the track record, almost like a horse possessed, his snout and tail parallel to the ground, his hooves chewing the dirt like a plow. I hardly noticed Grandpa pounding his hands together and the kid yelling "Go Mr. Ship!" All I could think as the horse rounded the track was "don't lose, Billy, please don't lose."

Andrews met me in the men's room after the race. He shook my hand and passed me a roll of bills. "That's some horse," he said.

I said, "He's unbeatable."

Later that night I looked at the money. The kid and Grandpa were safe across town, tucked in their own beds. Billy slept sprawled on the ground; head, mane, and feet tangled in the sweet hay—his after-race ritual. The horse pen was quiet. I assumed, if anything, Andrews had shorted me, but I unraveled six 100 dollar bills. I tried to put the money in my wallet, but my hands were shaking.

———

I should have never doubted him. Billy Ship couldn't lose. The local races. The regionals. It was the Sport of Kings, and Billy was the prince. He started to gain a national reputation. Different kind of people showed up at his track workouts. Rich men with cigars and big rings on thick fingers. Men in suits and dark sunglasses. Suede cowboy hats. The trainer said Billy was a shoo-in to qualify for the Breeders' Cup Juvenile. Next year he could run the big races with the three-year-olds. He would be worth more money than a man could dream of.

Uneasiness came along with Billy's success. Bigger padlocks on the door. A sheriff cruiser at sundown. The boss gave me a cell phone. He said to always have it on when I slept in the pen. He'd call three or four times a night. Sometimes he thought he heard yelling in the distance or squealing tires. Other times he claimed a car drove by his house a little too slowly. He would have slept in the stable himself, but the horse preferred me. No more vacation days, either. Billy couldn't sleep without me. He'd snort and pace and kick his feet. I was his nightlight.

Over time, I grew fond of that horse. He was the closest thing I had seen to perfection in my lifetime. Like a new car, flawless, no wear and tear. Even when they pushed him hard, he only seemed to get stronger, like he wanted it more. He wanted to win. He wanted to show the other horses how fast he could run. I loved that about him. His competitiveness, his arrogance, his unwilling-ness to lose. It reminded me of my grandpa—the way I imagined him in the old days, the good days. The days before he stopped believing he could do anything.

But Billy wasn't invincible. The workouts eventually started to hurt him. I remember one night when he sauntered over to my cot and lay down on his belly. He had strained a leg in practice that day and refused to put weight on it. I reached and touched his strong back, felt the muscles underneath. I could feel the blood pulsing, the flesh tightening, the nerves ready to explode. But Billy was asleep. At least, he slept as long as my hand was there. When I pulled away, he opened his eyes, turned his head, and stared. As soon as I put my hand back, his eyes closed. We repeated the pro-cess three or four times, until, finally, I swung one of my socked feet and rested it on his haunch. That was good enough for him. Right then, he seemed more like a puppy. A scared little kid. Not one of the fastest horses in the country. I almost liked him better that way.

What happened to Billy could have been fate. It may have been one of those times where so many little things go wrong in order for a big wrong to take place. People were losing too much money on his legs, or people were winning too much. Somebody called his number: a predator loan shark, an overextended bookie, a jealous thoroughbred owner, or maybe just an ordinary guy who lost more than he could bear. Whoever it was decided Billy could no longer win. When I think back on it now, I remember the time at the track with the kid and Grandpa. The look on Grandpa's face. The money I wagered—my own money, as if Billy was a sure thing. I don't know much about Charlie's friend Andrews. I don't know where his connections went, how deeply he was in. I didn't know who his friends were, what they were capable of. All I know is the confidence I showed on that one night might have been the reason those men came to get Billy Ship. It could have been me.

———

The boss told me never to leave the stable after dark, but Donna called in a frantic state. Please, please let the kid stay with you. Just for tonight. That's what she kept saying. She was on her last warning at work, and her mother was out of town, and there was no one else but me. If she didn't show, they'd fire her. Without a job, she was finished. They might as well take the kid. Declare her unfit. She wouldn't call if it weren't such an emergency.

I said, "Sure, just for tonight." And when I said it I dreamed of falling asleep in our old house. The kid down the hall. The thermostat turned down on a hot night. Donna stepping into the bedroom wearing one of my old baseball shirts, the hallway lights making her a silhouette in the doorway. I was never one for fancy lingerie, just wanted something soft against my hands. Something easy to take off. Or nothing at all.

But I missed more than that about Donna. I missed the smell of her shampoo, her kisses goodnight. I missed her telling the kid to call me dad, even though I hadn't earned it. When I think back on it now, it wasn't really Donna that I wanted. I missed the kid, the house. I missed pretending to be a family. Microwave popcorn, doing dishes, tv dinners. All that. I was sorry for not respecting her, sorry I didn't tell her she looked pretty when she dyed her hair or wore a dress, sorry I yelled in her face when she told me I needed to keep a job I hated for her and the kid, not for me. I was sorry I pretended to sleep when she wanted to talk about getting pregnant.

Over the phone, she asked if I could be there in twenty minutes. Of course I could. Her voice grew softer, and she said she was off tomorrow. I could come over if I wanted. I could bring something to drink.

"You know I'll be there," I said. "I'm still in love with you."

She told me not to talk that way.

"You could say it," I said. "It won't hurt you."

She kissed me that night, right after I knocked on the door. It felt like a reflex. She was headed out, and I was in her way. She touched her hand to my chest, reached up and found my lips, and that was our last kiss. The same night those men came to kill Billy Ship.

The kid was excited when I buckled him in the front seat of the Stingray. "We really get to sleep in a barn with a horse?"

"Right," I said, still buzzing from the kiss. "Don't tell your mom."

I don't know if those men picked the backdoor lock, or if I left it open by mistake. I didn't see them until we walked into the back stable, where Billy and I slept. There they were: three big men dressed in hooded gray sweatshirts. Six large gloved hands. One held a carving knife. The others steadied the reins.

They had draped a blindfold over Billy's eyes. He might have thought he was being prepped for a race. His ears twitched, and he shook his head to and fro, like he was loosening up.

"Take it easy," the man with the knife said to me. "No sense getting hurt over this."

There was nothing I could do to help Billy. That was clear. Somebody had come to pay the horse back for money lost. I stood there with the kid's head tucked into the crook of my arm so he couldn't see. It didn't seem real, more like a dream, but I couldn't wake up.

"Can't you let him go?" I said. "I'll drive him to the mountains. Tonight if I have to. He'll never race again."

"That's not an option," the man said. "No matter what, this is getting done."

I held up my hands. "I got a boy here."

"We're just going to cut him," the man said. "It's up to your trainer whether or not to put him down."

I nodded, turned to the kid.

"Look that way," I said. "Plug your ears for me."

The kid did as he was told. I should have plugged my ears, too. I should have looked away. All I could think about were the muscles in Billy Ship's legs, how useful they were, how strong, how they seemed to do exactly what they needed to do. I was trapped between the kid and the horse. My arms hung limp—shoulders, legs, and hands—all useless. There were so many things I couldn't do. I couldn't get Donna back. I couldn't stop Grandpa from dying. I couldn't keep a job to save my life, let alone my car. If I had Billy's strength, I could have stopped the men. I could have fought all three and won, might have even killed them. But I'm not like him. He didn't know how to lose. He didn't know what it means to try, and fail, and keep going. That's all I know how to do.

I knelt down and held the kid, who didn't yet understand what was happening. It wouldn't be long before he turned his head, unplugged his ears, and looked at me in disbelief. He'd want to know, who were those men? Why was I sad? How could I let those terrible things happen to the horse?

THREE MONTHS

The day before my brother reported to county jail to serve his ninety-day sentence, we kayaked the back flats of Big Creek Lake. It's a small body of water, more like a finger lake than anything, attached by a concrete causeway to the big reservoir that fills the land northwest of Des Moines, Iowa. One of his favorite spots, he said. I remember the sun rising across the lake's surface as we paddled along the forest shore, each in his own kayak. The only sound was breathing, and blades dipping in and out. I was the lead. The white fiberglass of my boat cut through algae and froth. My brother hung back, took things slow. He stole extra time that day: beaching his kayak on the shore to grab a hollow can or hunk of trash, stopping under the shade of an overhanging tree. He hated to see the sun move across the sky.

My brother is a sweet man. This is what my wife says, and the girls he brings home sometimes to meet Mom and Dad, but he turns into a different person when his temper rises. After his arrest, he was charged with three misdemeanors and a felony assault. My brother, charged with a felony. That doesn't sound real, but it was. He broke two bones in some kid's face. The other lawyer said the kid won't ever look right. People won't recognize him because of what my brother did.

I don't believe that. Flesh, bones, blood. Everything heals eventually.

The judge went soft on my brother, mostly because he was a

second grade teacher. Some of the other teachers stood character witness. They filled the courtroom with their support. You should have seen the young one—the music teacher who he slept with spring semester. She cried so hard after the sentencing, you'd think he was condemned to die. No one knew if she was actually upset, or if she was upset at herself for sleeping with a man who would spend a season of his life behind bars. They fired him, though, despite the felony getting dropped, despite a formal apology to the kid with the destroyed face. He wouldn't hug anybody when it was over, not Mom, not my wife, not the music teacher. I don't think I would have hugged him, either, if he had reached for me.

"So, what do people do while they're in there?" I pulled my kayak alongside his. He was staring off toward the shore where a painted turtle lounged on a half-sunk log. Its long neck stretched toward the sun.

"I don't know. I heard they play a lot of cards," he said.

"Lift weights."

"No, that's prison. Prison's where you lift weights. That's for killers and rapists. I'm not going there."

"I didn't know there was a difference."

"There is. Trust me," he said.

We pushed through the gap in the earth dam, made our way into the silt. The lake continued north through the trees to Madrid, but it was only a foot deep, if that. Mud brushed the bottom of the kayak. I sunk an oar in the water. Only half the blade went down before mush. My brother paddled off toward the west end where three or four Canadians slept, heads backward, bills hidden in wing feathers.

"I'm bottomed out," I called. "You?"

"I don't know," he said. He pushed his paddle hard into the lake, splashing brown water and silt with each stroke.

"It's too shallow to keep going," I said.

Then something happened I didn't expect. Maybe I did. My brother pressed his face into his hands and began to cry. I hadn't seen him do that since we were little kids. He thought I couldn't see him (he had his back to me), but I could. He wasn't making a show of it. If you didn't know him, you'd think he was shielding his eyes from the sun.

What do you say to a brother who's headed for jail? It's only ninety days. Or is it better to think of it as three months? A quarter year?

————

I'm not a brave man, but people say I saved my brother's life when I was sixteen. My brother was thirteen. I didn't think about it when it happened. The situation presented itself, and I responded.

We were hiking the grass field behind Sandpiper boat ramp with our Lab, Duke. Duke was getting old, so we took him out to chase pheasants and quail whenever we could. Nothing too special about the sky that day, just a few clouds, maybe a touch darker than normal. Might be a storm later on, I thought, but no thunder, no lightning. Walking back to the truck it started to sprinkle, and then a few fat drops of rain. Then it was hard rain. We moved quicker, but we were still a mile from the truck when the first hailstone fell. It landed on the ground with a little thud, looking out of place like a fish that accidentally flipped itself onto shore.

If we didn't know what was coming, we probably would have picked up the hail and inspected it. We ran, but there was no way to make it. No trees in sight. Just us and grass.

I remember Duke snapping at the hail stones, trying to catch them in his mouth. They were mostly little at first. One stung his snout, and he took off yelping. Somehow, that dog avoided the worst of it. Dad found him the next day, skulking along the highway. There were several spots of dried blood on his back, but other than that, nothing.

When the hail started to get bigger, I didn't think, I just pulled my brother down into the grass. I covered my head with coat and hands, and spread myself over the top of him like a shield. Most of the hail were golf ball size. A few were like baseballs.

"Lemme go," my brother yelled from underneath.

"Shut up and stay down," I said.

The thing about the hail, really, is that I went numb after a while. When you get hit with a rock, you have time to think about it and process the pain. When you get hit by rock after rock after rock, there's not much time to think. The storm lasted maybe thirty or forty-five seconds. My brother said I screamed my head off. The doctor said I surely passed out. My brother squirmed underneath the whole time, trying to get free, but I held him tight.

The hail broke two of my ribs and four fingers. Welts covered my hamstrings, my calves, a terrible purple patch on the left side of my neck. When they brought me in, the doctor thought I had been beaten with a club.

"You shouldn't have done that," my brother said to me. "I'm not made of glass."

Later, when we were on shore, my cell phone rang. I walked out of earshot. My brother was loading the kayaks into the pickup.

"Why can't I be there?" my wife asked over the phone.

"You don't want to be there, trust me," I said. "We're just going to hang out at his house. Probably get drunk."

"You act like I don't matter," she said.

"Of course you do," I said into the phone. Right now, though, she didn't matter. Not to my brother. Not to the next twenty-two hours.

"If you guys drink alcohol, you should stay home," she said. "Tonight would be a terrible night for him to get in trouble."

"I need to hang up now," I said.

Being there that night wasn't a privilege. No way I'd let my wife be a part of it. Mom and Dad said they couldn't. They couldn't watch their son go to jail. Dad pored over his decision for days. Finally, he decided on a phone call.

I can imagine the phone conversation—short and to the point. "I want you to come back from this stronger than before." Dad said that to me when Ted Phillips, my good friend, drowned in the Des Moines River. Ted wasn't a strong swimmer, and he got caught in

31

the currents trying to cross in the flood. It was a race. The rest of us made the west shore fine, but Ted never showed on the other side. One moment there were six boys paddling as fast as we could, the next it was five. There wasn't any struggle or yelling. There weren't any signs. He just disappeared.

Dad told me to take my time. Find a way to deal with it. He said he wanted me to come back a stronger person.

─────

The tv was on the whole night. I don't think my brother slept. We split a case of beer, but didn't get through six or seven . There was too much silence in the room. What do you talk about? I started off nice. "When you get out," I said, "a trip to New Orleans. You and me."

I thought he'd run with it. We'd talk about how would we get there. Drive, fly, train? We'd decide which CDs to bring, what kind of food to eat. But he didn't talk about that. He said something about New Orleans being swept underwater in Hurricane Katrina. He couldn't stand to see all that water damage. He recalled watching the news: folks dying in the flood, folks waving their arms from rooftops, the bodies of folks clogging the sewers. Perhaps there was a man still alive off sewer rats, he said, and dogs that used to be household pets gnashing their teeth and running wild in packs. A fucking nightmare. And then there were the people, idiot Creoles, drinking mint juleps and Abita beer, dancing around in confetti-filled streets as if the hurricane never happened. They tried to pretend their world hadn't changed, but it had. Why couldn't they accept it?

My brother didn't understand. To him, three months in jail was as good as dead. But he was too young. He didn't know that time moved on, wounds healed. People forgive you, even if you wrecked their face. Even if you slept with a girl, a sweet girl, and then ruined it by committing a felony. How can you explain to your parents that you let a felon inside you? What if you carried a felon's child?

Your mom and dad, your family and friends. They forgive you too, over time, because you don't really change. Not in your core. If you love somebody once, you love them for the rest of your life. That's what I believe. I've seen it happen. Who cries harder: the widow, or the ex-wife at a man's funeral? Who cries harder in private?

My brother didn't cry that night; he only cried at the lake, when he thought I wasn't looking, when it was just him and God and the Canadian geese to judge. I didn't feel sorry. He was finally getting what he deserved. Some of us go through life and we don't lose our tempers. We don't swing our fists at people's faces with a purpose of breaking bones. We don't challenge people to box, even when we're drunk, even when we feel blood-full veins, and we're charged as lightning, and the girls will be so excited if we strut like we're ever so tough. Some of us aren't like that.

We were up at dawn. No reason to get there early, was the only thing he said about it before we hit the road. He wore a pair of blue jeans and an old high school sweatshirt, his eyes hid under dark sunglasses.

When we reached the corner where left was jail and right was straight out toward the interstate and 1500 miles between each coast, he said what I had expected him to say all along. "Man, take a right and keep going, don't stop." He wasn't kidding.

"No, I won't," I said. But I thought about it. Juvenile thoughts. Turn right now, punch the gas, and we're headed east. 500 feet between us and the onramps. Don't look in the rearview until the sign says "Welcome to Illinois." Or take the left exit, burn a dust trail through Nebraska and Colorado. Hit the Rockies before dark. But then what? Head for the border? This wasn't a bunch of snot-nosed kids playing hide and seek. If he didn't show they'd sentence him to real time, hard time. Ready or not, your felony's back. Here's one to three in Leavenworth.

I said, "We're getting this done."

33

"We aren't doing anything. I'm checking into jail. Me."

"Three months is nothing. I'll be there to pick you up."

"Can you stop, for one minute, all this talk about three months from now? Three months from now this. Three months from now that," he said. "It's not three months from now. It's right now. This is where I'm at."

I drove slowly, I really did, but we pulled into the county jail parking lot well before 8 o clock. It didn't look like a prison. My brother was right. It looked more like an office building with brick walls, and an American flag out front. There was some sort of cop or guard through the front door, and my brother said he had to surrender himself to that man at the top of the hour.

"Do you say, 'I give up'?" I asked. My brother didn't laugh. He stared at the entrance. I would like to think he looked resolved, but he looked more confused than anything. Maybe he didn't believe it was happening.

"Well," he said. "I better get going."

He shook my hand. I squeezed it before I let go. He set his sunglasses on the dash, and then he was out the door, walking down the sidewalk toward the entrance. I could see the officer on the inside, looking through the window. I didn't think to walk him there. His head was down the whole way, but his shoulders were up. The officer opened the entrance door, and I wanted to see my brother look back, just once, so I could give him a wave or a thumbs up or even look him in the eye before the door closed, and I would never see him again. Of course, I would, ninety days later, but he wouldn't be the same person he was right then, taking it all in like a man, more of a man than me, because the truth is that I was stuck to the truck seat. I couldn't move a muscle. My heart was broken, and it wasn't the obvious thing. The obvious thing would have been the hail storm, how I had laid on top of him, saved him from getting hurt. The obvious thing would have been to compare the two situations, and see that there was nothing I could do to protect him now, not even sacrifice myself. It would have been predictable for me to wonder why I bothered saving him, if this is how he would repay me. But I wasn't thinking about that. Stupid me. I was thinking about my brother's birthday, the year before. We had split a couple pitchers of Boulevard and a basket of chicken wings. He had said, next year, he would like to go camping. A full-fledged camping trip, just me and him, maybe a few of our best friends. We could catch trout in the stream, wrap the fish in foil and bacon; throw them right on the coals. That's what he wanted. No tents, no cell phones. Just our wits and sleeping bags. We should really do it, he had said. Have one great birthday weekend before everybody gets old and has kids and mortgages and problems. We should do it not just for him, but for me, too. I needed it as badly as he did.

I remember him saying those words exactly. He had barbeque sauce on his lips, and that rasp in his voice you get from talking in a loud bar. It was one of those honest moments you share, when a person tells you precisely what he is longing for. You could almost look through his eyes, stare directly into his daydream. We rarely tell the truth about what we really want. I don't know why.

That's what got me: thinking about my brother's 25th birthday. He would still be inside, still trapped. Maybe they would let him out for the weekend. They could put a little break into his sentence, spring him for good behavior. I knew they never would.

What happened next was predictable. The door closed. I shut my eyes.

MOUNTAIN PASSING

Snow continues to fall on the car. The windshield, wet and warm from the defrost, melts the flakes on impact. Robert engages the wipers and the blades slick away the wetness. He has stopped talking, now, but sound continues: Belle's heavy breathing, sniffing, and the soft buzz of heat vents.

Inside the car, the word *they* is over. Robert is driving Belle's car back to Denver. She is riding along. When he arrives, he and his clothes will take a cab to his apartment, and she will lock her bedroom door. She will light a votive and watch it melt into nothing, like she always does when she loses something before she is ready to let it go.

Robert steers the car through the mountains, holding it tight around the curves. The tires spin, inconsequential in the whiteness. Yesterday, when he and she were together, they slept naked under a blanket. She told him that she had kissed a girl once, the way the French do. It was kind of like kissing him, she said, but softer. He asked her to tell him more, but she had already fallen asleep. They woke sweat-covered, the fire in embers, his skin sunburn warm and red, the area between his legs grown cold.

Belle's car is the only vehicle on the road, except for the old snowplow. The diesel engine leads the way, releasing silver smoke. The car's tires wade through the smoothed snow left by the plow's blade. Robert follows the red winking taillights, knowing he is 150 miles from Denver, going fifteen miles an hour, with two-thirds of a tank of gas.

He has decided, if the car gives out, or the tires catch ice and then ditch, he will open the door, leave the keys, and walk out to the tree line. Douglas Firs and Ponderosa Pines can survive blizzards of all magnitudes, and so can he. He will dig a cocoon in the snow, like a sled dog, until he is a pocket of warmth beneath the cold. If Belle can find him, he will share his heat with her, he will let his hands and the words only said in claustrophobic quarters slide over her like bath water. He will allow her to love him again. But she will never find him.

He fiddles with the radio, twisting the knobs in hope of finding an AM weather station. She tells him it doesn't work, never has. The damn thing was broken from the moment she bought it.

———

They had arrived at the cabin the day before with different intentions. She had intended to hear him say the words "I love you" for the first time, and he had intended to make love to her on every flat surface. He did love her, too, but he would never realize this until she showed it to him in a way he could understand, like waking him up in a gentle fashion—stroking the hardness in his boxer shorts or bringing him a cup of coffee in the nude.

In the afternoon, she decided to initiate the secret game. The rules were simple. She started out by sharing a secret that was small, and he had to outdo her with a secret of higher consequence.

"If I was a rich girl, I would hoard all my money and never work," she said. "And I'd have all kinds of plastic surgery."

Robert said, "When I see a person at a movie or a restaurant all by himself, it makes me want to cry."

"I cried when I lost my virginity," Belle said, "but I didn't cry when my stepfather died."

———

The night turns lightless. The road curves between two mountains,

37

then rises. Evergreen trees line both sides of the pass like sage and brown pylons. To the left, a stream cuts a wet trail through the whiteness, too warm and too fast to freeze. The wind has lightened, but the snow falls harder, in clumps now. Robert uses the wipers to sweep it away. His speed has dropped to a crawl. If this car can make it to I-70, he thinks, it will be a clear shot to Denver. The big plows will be all over the interstate, pushing the snow away, making the path clean. For now, though, he must rely on the old diesel plow as it chugs up the incline, leading the way like a hobbled tour guide.

"If we get stuck and freeze to death," she says, "it's your fault."

"We aren't going to get stuck."

"We could have stayed another night, in the cabin with a fireplace, but now we are driving in the car through a blizzard."

"You were the one that said we had to leave."

"Because of you. We had to leave because of you."

"We aren't going to get stuck," Robert says.

He presses the brake. There is no shoulder to park in—no road really, except for the strip cleared by the plow. He opens the door; she asks, "What are you doing?"

"I have to go," he says. He puts on his gloves and hat.

As he stands up, cold stings the inside of his nose. Drops of snow brush his face, stick to his eyelashes. He turns toward the tree line; tries to unzip his jeans, but realizes he must first take off his gloves. The wind bites his bare hands. He sets the gloves on top of the car, undoes his pants, and urinates quickly in the darkness. He closes his eyes and feels the cold against his exposed skin; takes a deep breath and lets it out. When he gets back into the car, the seat next to his is empty. The door is open. Belle is gone.

Robert removes his hat. He grips the steering wheel and stares up the road, straight ahead. He shuts off the wipers. The snow begins to cover the windshield. Two minutes go by, then two more. The flakes fall on the glass, stacking up like little white shovelfuls. The windshield becomes a blank sheet – a cave of snow, he thinks, in which he can hide long enough to breathe himself to death.

Yesterday, when he and Belle lay next to the fireplace, he pulled the blankets overhead. In the darkness, Belle's body inched closer. He felt her face against his.

We're going to suffocate, she said.

There's plenty of air under here.

She kissed his fingertips. It's not worth it, she said. I can't breathe. And it's too dark.

It's a good kind of dark.

He turns his head when he hears the passenger door close. Belle sits back down and buckles her seat belt. "I had to go too," she says in a quiet voice. She reaches over, switches the wipers back on, and points to the plow's distant taillights. "Hurry, we can't let him get away."

———

Robert had felt coldness between his legs when he woke, naked. The rest of his skin was covered in sweat, red from the heat of the dying fire. Belle's eyes were open above him, taking in his features. The mess of her auburn hair fell around his face.

"It's my turn to tell you a secret," she said.

"You told me a secret last night. Before you fell asleep. You said that you made out with a girl."

"Kissed," she said. "I kissed a girl. There's a difference, you know. And that's not a real secret. I have something else I want to tell you. Something better."

She took his hands. He felt her thin fingers beneath his. She said, "The real secret is that I am falling in love with you, and I am afraid to say it. I figured if we played the secret game, then you would end up telling me you loved me, and I wouldn't be afraid anymore. But you haven't said anything, yet. So, I am going to tell you, right now, that I am in love with you. That's my secret." She paused. Her fingers squeezed. "And now it's your turn."

Robert closed his eyes. He had known this moment would come, but he kept figuring it would be the next day, and then the day after that. He let go of her hands. "Before I tell you," he said, "there's one more thing I have to share. It's not a big deal, but I need to let you know this one thing first."

He could see it in her face. Even before he started the story, he knew that it would be a big deal to her, it would come down on her like too much weight and she would wilt to the ground like a plant with a broken stem. But he had to say it—he had been sleeping with another girl when he and Belle first started dating, a casual thing that he only kept alive for the first three weeks, until the sparks started to fly between him and Belle, but he had never told her. He never told either of them. As far as Belle knew, he was as single as she was the first time they kissed, but he had made love to someone else the night before. That was Robert's secret.

————

Silence fills the car. She has stopped crying, stopped talking, stopped trying to make things right or make him wrong. He doesn't want this ending though, trapped between mountains of snow with no words of kindness. The only thing for him to do is steer the car. He can follow the snowplow until the foothills open and Denver's lights shine through, he thinks, or even until the end of time, but he cannot handle all this silence.

He remembers something he said to Belle when they first started dating. They had been standing on the stoop of his apartment complex. He fumbled for the keys, while she shook in the cold and complained of hypothermia. He told her, people who freeze to death become numb over time. They feel quite warm when they die, but the beginning hurts much more. Well, I am definitely beginning to die, she said. She pressed her body against his, snuggled against his pea coat. If I go, she said, I'm taking you with me. He hugged her back before opening the door, noticing for the first time how much smaller she was than him; how soft she felt when dressed in wool and fleece; and how he could lift her off her feet, spin her around and breathe the scent of her hair as if she weighed nothing at all.

He shivers and runs a hand through his own hair. He starts to talk. "My family was really poor, one Christmas, when I was in junior high school," he says. "My dad was laid off at the plant, and my mom hadn't gotten her job at the bank yet. My brothers were all home from college, and my uncle was in town, too. You remember them all, don't you?"

She doesn't answer.

"Anyway, this terrible storm came through town that night when everybody got in. It was kind of like this storm, only worse. Late in the afternoon, it started to rain, and the birch trees in our backyard got soaked, but then the temperature dropped, and the rain turned to ice. When I opened the sliding door, I could hear tree limbs breaking, but I couldn't see anything. The wind was so bad, like a highway of ice and snow and sleet in my face. The ice took down half the town's power lines.

"My mom made us all go downstairs. Our basement was semi-finished, half carpeted—we used it mostly for storage. The rug was all worn out. Against the south wall, we had this old wood burning stove. It was black, probably weighed 400 pounds; looked like a squat, iron animal hunched in the corner. The stove had a glass door. My dad put that on when I was a kid, so we could watch the fire burn inside. That night in the storm, we laid out blankets and quilts next to the stove, me and my brothers, all of us watching the logs in the stove's belly turn to ash, like when we were little kids. There wasn't much to look at, because wood stoves don't give off much light. Nobody talked. We just lay in the warmth and watched the fire.

"My parents and my uncle sat behind us in folding chairs, drinking coffee. I found out, later, that my mom was crying back there in the dark, because she didn't have enough money to buy us presents, only stocking stuffers, which she charged to her credit card. I was mad about it at the time, because I didn't want us to be poor, but I shouldn't have been. I hate myself for that. I wish I could take it back.

"The next morning, when I went outside, all the birch trees were sagged, bent over, their top branches flush with the ground. It looked like their hearts had stopped in the cold."

When he glances over, Belle is facing the window, watching

the snow fall.

————

Ahead, brake lights flash, and the snowplow comes to a halt. The car is on the downslope, close to the crest of a low lying peak. "Shit," Robert says. He pulls the car up behind the parked plow and waits. "Something's wrong," he says. The downfall has lightened, but the wind has picked back up. It sweeps at the tracks in the road, blows tilt-o-whirls across the headlights.

The snowplow's door opens. The outline of a large figure steps out—a big man with a ponytail. The plowman takes a step or two away from his vehicle, lights a cigarette. The drift comes up to his knees. Robert cannot see his features. The cigarette's orange cherry glows where the face should be.

Robert continues to wait—five, ten minutes. He does not want to get out of the car. The idea of standing face to face with the large shadow of the plowman scares him. He would rather be on the interstate, moving forward at fifty, sixty miles an hour, moving toward Denver. He looks into Belle's eyes; she wants him to do something, wants him to find out what is wrong, but she does not want to make him go, because she is afraid, too. The inside of the car is safe, Robert thinks, but there is no going back the way they came. The blizzard has buried the tracks and covered the roads. It is too dark, and mountains look the same at night. All he knows is that he has been driving north and east toward the interstate, and he cannot drive unless the plow clears the path.

After he gets out of the car, he can see Belle's face pressed against the windshield, trying to watch. The wind pulls at his coat as he struggles forward through the drifts. He realizes that he left his gloves on top of the car when he stopped to go to the bathroom. The gloves are gone, blown away and lost somewhere in the night. He shakes his head and pockets his cold hands.

As he comes up from behind, the shape of the plowman becomes bigger and bigger. He is dressed in flannel and jeans, coatless. The ponytail hangs down to the middle of his back, bound every couple of inches by rubber bands. The size of the plowman's calloused hands makes Robert keep his distance.

"You hung up?" asks Robert. The plowman turns his head. He is in his fifties, thick-necked, scarred, leather-skinned but clean-shaven. Blue eyes. He takes a drag on his cigarette and holds it out at arm's length. At first Robert thinks he is flicking the ash, but then he realizes the plowman is telling him to look forward, where the cigarette points.

There are at least fifty of them. Bighorn sheep. Some are less than fifteen yards away. The snow is up to their chins. They move slowly, hoof over hoof, across the mountain pass. The rams lead the way, heads down—their proud, curving horns glazed in ice; their breath crystallizing in steampuffs between their thick knees. They push their way through the snow. The spike-horned ewes bring up the rear, stepping where the males have broken trail.

The only sound is wind, no snort or wavering bleat. In the head-lights, the brown, coarse coats hang like blankets on the sheep's backs. The flurries beat against them, sticking to matted ears and eyelids. In the middle of the flock, the hornless, adolescent lambs, half the size of the rams, shake in the cold. Their steps are less sure, less strong. The lambs swim, ears deep, in the high drifts, kicking and bounding to get to shallower snow.

Off to the left, the leader—a barrel-necked ram—stands above the snow on the impossible slope of a boulder. His tremendous horns curl in a thick helmet around his face. The rest of the big-horns are cold and tired, but not this one. His legs, like thick trunks of veins, hold him steady on the slick rock. He puffs his chest and raises his white-dipped muzzle toward the falling snowflakes, searches the black clouds for some sign of moonlight. He opens his lips and the sound of his vibrato call wavers through the pass. The bighorns bleat in response. Some pause to chew the snow, others lift their heads and continue forward. The first rams make the edge of the road. They disappear into the pines.

"Never seen them like this, so many," the plowman says, his voice like rocks rubbed together. "Don't know what got into that big son-of-a-bitch, but he sure thinks they ought to be somewhere

43

else right now."

Robert nods. He does not know, either. Oblivious to the cold, his unpocketed hands hang limply at his sides. He and the plowman stand in silence, watching the sheep struggle through the pass. Belle is out of the car, now, the sound of her footsteps approaching. She shivers. "They look like ghosts crossing a white river," she says. "They won't freeze, will they?"

"They'll be okay," the plowman says. "They're tough as hell."

Robert feels soft cloth against his numbing fingers. He looks down. Belle's mitten squeezes his bare hand.

THE PITCHER

This happens about the same time the heat moves into the area. It makes everything worse. The sun dead-stops in the sky overhead and doesn't move for a month. At first it is one simple, cloudless day of ninety-eight degrees, but then the days keep coming, waves of drought with no relief in sight. Fifteen without rain, clouds, or breeze, then eighteen, then twenty. The cold fronts that push through Middle America forget their way. A haze covers the Great Plains horizon. Conversations begin and end with the same question: "Can you believe this heat?" Hospitals beds fill with cases of exhaustion and stroke. The patience of the city sags to the thinness of paper. The skin of pissed off residents burns sun-red. Domestic disputes skyrocket. The city asks road construction crews to work the night shift. On television, weathermen plead with the elderly and parents of small children. Everybody, everywhere is just burning, burning, burning like ants on asphalt.

In the middle of the heat a man, the pitcher, is rinsing the tips of his fingers in dirt and licking dry lips. A woman curls her painted toes into the cement amongst peanut shells and sunflower casings. People are yelling his name, but she doesn't hear them. He—the pitcher, Jeremy Dove—knows that if he doubts the strength in his shoulder for even a moment, if his elbow bends a touch convex, the stadium lights will flicker and dim, the screams will fade into nothing, and she—his girlfriend, Eloise Ann, who sits for him above the west end of the visitor's dugout—will be gone. Four days out of the week she doesn't love him the way he wants her to, but every fifth day he is a star. Every fifth day he is everything she needs him to be.

The irony is he doesn't like baseball, not really, not the way he used to when he was a talented eight-year-old chewing the fat with his friends in a dusty, chain-link dugout. Everything is different now. This is a job—a livelihood of desiccated throat and frayed nerves—but when he wins, Eloise Ann meets him at the edge of the stadium, presses against him as if he were the ground and she were the setting sun. Moments pass and she is in his bedroom, swimming in sheets. The hem of her t-shirt rises over unbuttoned jeans, then above her head. She is his wet miracle, his much needed rainfall. Every fifth day they are happy. Before the hollowness of morning and heat's return, nights move as if struck by a match.

———

This man is the size of a quarter horse, Eloise Ann thought on the day they met. She leaned forward when she set his bone-dry cappuccino on the table, allowing the cut of her blue tank to hang like a window before him. He was tanned as copper, tower tall, and broad of shoulder and hip. She hadn't noticed him until the third person approached his table, a young kid with a baseball, and she watched him turn and sign the ball awkwardly, skirting the room's attention. He was halfway through the morning paper, handsome in the way that soldiers with buzzed hair and fitted t-shirts are handsome in dedication. She liked the tangled ruggedness of his hair and five o' clock shadow, how his veins compelled his forearms, and how his dimensions seemed to dwarf the normal-sized men standing in line for their morning espressos.

His newspaper dropped when the plated scone clicked on the table, and she smiled hoping to make him suddenly forget where he was. She didn't normally flirt with customers, but there was something about this guy. She wanted closeness, a filling desire to hear the deepness of his voice and smell the clean tickle of his cologne. She couldn't help but wonder how quickly a man of his size could undress her.

"I didn't buy this," he said.

"I made it for you," she said. "Try it."

"Oh," he said, face flushing, and took a bite with the same uncomfortable manner in which he had signed the baseball.

"It's good. Thank you." He turned back to the paper.

She retreated behind the counter, abashed at her forwardness. She was the type of girl who received attention when she wanted it, and rejection tasted foreign in her mouth. Restless, she started a light roast drip and began to froth a triple latte.

The next time she looked up he was standing in front of her.

"If I leave you a ticket at Will Call, will you watch me play tonight?"

She wanted to nod, but instead balanced her palms against the counter. A player of some kind, an athlete. She knew little about athletes. Athletes understood what it was like to have strangers cheer for them. Men lived and died by an athlete's work. Kids idolized them, and she had heard stories of this woman or that woman, from time to time, letting an athlete do to her whatever he wanted just because he was an athlete, and that's what athletes do.

"I only have one ticket," he said.

She wondered why this felt like the knot of a blindfold unraveling. Why did she feel seconds away from staring into the faces of a crowded room?

Every fifth day the pitcher gets a hundred chances to force a man to swing and miss. By the time he hurls fifty, pins and needles numb his shoulder. By eighty, his elbow is warm to the touch and fingertips are lifeless—he can barely make out the seams. He knows, though, that there will be a bucket of ice in the dugout and cold beers in the bullpen catcher's hands, and, if he holds on to win, Eloise Ann will be there in his bedroom to disentangle the tension coursing through his body.

The heavyset sports analysts on the radio call him a three. He's not good enough to be a one or a two, but he's better than a four. Eloise Ann listens to them in her headphones as she jogs along the asphalt river trail. The voices on the radio use his name in terrible puns. They tar and feather him when his slider doesn't slide, when the balls go swooping in between gloves and soaring over the fence, and the pitcher gets chased in the fourth inning like a pigeon fleeing the crack of birdshot. In the dugout, he buries his face into the leather nest of glove, ears and hands ringing, shoulders shaking. Nobody talks to him, then, not even the pitching coach. He's beyond crestfallen.

But when he's on, the men on the radio sing his praises. Unhittable at times, they say, a chip on the old wing, possessed by the devil himself. He can shave both sides of a batter's face. He can take a club to the Promised Land. Eloise Ann finds herself breaking into a full trot when they talk about the pitcher with such reverence—her pitcher—the type of player franchises are built around. She could run the entire length of the river on those days.

The pitcher knows that if he presses a whisper harder with his middle finger on the right seam of a ball, the pitch will cut toward the wrist of a left-handed bat. If he squeezes his index finger, the ball will float right and jam a right-hander at the plate. He can paint corners, throw a circle-change, and drop the table off a slider. It's all natural to him: touch, feel, and instincts. There are no physics involved. His fastball clocks ninety-three miles an hour, which is off the charts for most humans. Ninety-three miles an hour can get you through extended spring training, the independent leagues, even high A ball, but once you hit double A, prospects see everything. You need craft and grit, the ability to second guess yourself and confuse the batter. Even then, only the best of the best drink more than a cup of coffee in the major leagues. The fat analysts on the radio say the pitcher has "stuff," but he needs to establish a cerebral connection to the game. Right now, he's only a thrower.

He threw hard enough once to end a man's career. It was an accident that most will forget—a veteran player with a beard sinking like a hedge off his face, swinging out his last couple days as a

48

designated hitter.

The pitch almost ended the veteran's life. In the aftermath, the DH lay on the dirt with one arm hobbled under the bat and the other draped over the plate. The crowd fell silent. The jumbotron flickered mute, and the players took a knee. The trainer clapped his hands hard over the injured player. "Wake up, Barnsie," he said. "Open your eyes." The pitcher turned to the outfield wall, face hidden in glove. He couldn't talk. He couldn't wet his lips. He certainly couldn't look.

Eloise Ann had never wanted him so badly as that night. There was a mania about him. She imagined him stalking the hotel room in his undershirt, watching highlights on television, jabbering away to her on his cell phone. He asked if he should call the batter to apologize, but she said absolutely not. He had done everything right, perfectly in fact. She squeezed a pillow between her legs.

"Don't talk," she said. "Just breathe into the phone. I want to hear you breathe."

She closed her eyes, and in her mind she pictured rivers of water emptying into the ocean.

————

The Children's Place Hospital became the baseball club's charity of choice in the early nineties, and the pitcher was contractually obligated to make an appearance one Saturday a month. On his first visit the nurse, a heavy-shouldered black woman, told him that some of the kids in the hospital would never make it to the age of ten and some of them would go onto live full lives. If he wanted to sleep easier at night, he might be better off never to find out which one was which.

Frankie B, a skinny thirteen-year-old with sharp elbows and a smart mouth, had been burned badly in a house fire. He lost critical skin mass on the majority of his left torso, arm, and leg. The nurses advised the pitcher to treat the left side of the kid's body like glass but the right side like stone. Give him a man's high five on the right, they said, but don't you dare touch him anywhere the fire did. The pitcher thought about the time his own forearm brushed a hot skillet, how the bubble of skin continued to burn even after ten minutes of running cool water over it.

"Francis, what's going on, man?" said Jeremy when he entered the burned kid's room.

"That's not my name, cocksucker."

The kid only had eyes for the wall. He wore a baseball hat on his head, cocked sideways. His lower half and left arm from the shoulder to wrist were wrapped in yellow gauze. The dressing was moist around the edges with cherry, crinkled skin peeking out—a boy king partially mummified.

From the hallway the nurse said, "He gets mad if people don't call him Frankie B."

"Frankie B. I like that."

"They sent me Dove? Not Ramon. Not Davis. Not even Johnson. I get Dove. "

"Could be worse. Could have sent Holloway."

"I guess that's true. So what do I get, Dove? A perfect game to stop me from croaking? Are you going to let me hold your sunflower seeds in the dugout?"

"Nurse said you used to play ball. Shortstop, right? You look like a shortstop. What did you bat?"

"I don't want to talk about me. Half my body looks like Betty White's ass. I ain't exactly lacing up the old cleats anytime soon. "

"What do you want to talk about, then?"

"I don't know. How come you don't pitch like an ace?"

"Who says I don't."

"I didn't question the size of your nuts, dude. I say you don't pitch like an ace. Jesus, your record says you don't. "

"It's the major leagues, little man. Everybody gets hit, even the aces."

"That's a horseshit answer."

"It's the truth."

"It's a horseshit answer."

The pitcher motioned for him to keep his voice down. "Alright, fine. Relax for Christ's sake. Sometimes I'm not that good, I guess.

Sometimes I throw over the plate as hard as I can and they still hit it out of the park. These guys are murderers. They hit everything. And then there are the ones who swing a lucky bat. That's the worst. The .220 hitters who hit you hard. People don't understand. The world hates a major league pitcher. Hitters could figure me out. I might start tipping pitches. Tommy John surgery. Torn rotator cuff. Guys like me get so many throws at this level, and when we string together enough bad ones, we become a footnote. Sent down. Career over."

"Is that it?"

 "What do you mean 'is that it'?"

"Don't you feel like killing them?"

"Who?"

"The guys who shouldn't hit your pitches but still do."

"I don't know. Not really killing them, no."

"Maybe that's your problem, Dove. I'd want to kill them. There's nothing wrong with me thinking that."

"Okay."

"Of course it's okay. That's just how I'd feel. We're allowed to feel any way we want."

The pitcher spent the next hour sitting in the chair next to Frankie B's bed, clicking buttons and twisting toggles, deeply focused on the grainy television bolted to the ceiling. Frankie B was a pro at the science-fiction, shoot-em-up videogame, and he sometimes would complete a level without firing a bullet, sneaking up on his enemies and braining them in the back of the head with the butt of his laser gun. The pitcher survived for maybe thirty seconds before he was gored horribly or incinerated by the evil aliens. After he died his character regenerated at the last checkpoint. By the time he would catch up to Frankie, all the bad guys were toast.

"See, we only gotta start the level over if we both die," Frankie said. "It's a real team sport."

"Good thing I have you on my team. I'm an embarrassment to this game."

"You should be used to that."

The pitcher tossed the controller to the foot of the bed. "Watch yourself, killer. That mouth is going to get you in trouble. Next homestand I'll come back. We'll tear those aliens a new one. I got to run now."

"Wait."

Jeremy paused in the doorway.

"My dick got cooked, you know. That doctor said my nerves won't come back, and I'll never be able to get hard."

––––––

The view of the world from the mound is reduced. It closes down, contracts, and refocuses as something more precise like a photograph rendered at smaller resolution. Sudden clarity takes shape through the fuzz. The pitcher knows what to do. He can feel the seams play against his fingertips – the unique whorls on his prints, no duplicate pattern in the world. A baseball at face value seems perfect and uniform—built to exact specification in a Louisville factory: two sewn together pieces of leather, 108 red rolled stitches of cotton thread, five ounces in weight. But if you measured the balls to a thousandth of a degree, a millionth, variance exists in weight, shape, and color.

A pitcher strives for uniformity. He tries to duplicate the motion every single time: the wind-up, the arm angle, the mask of the ball in glove, the follow-through, the elbow bend, the after-step. In order to survive, a major league pitcher must turn himself into a robot.

Like the baseballs, Eloise Ann could be handled with uniformity. She could be manipulated with a turn of the face, a tightening of one's fist at the small of her back, and a warm mouth dipping into the flesh above her shoulder. When the pitcher drinks deeply he feels her legs aching to curl around him. He knows what to do. He knows how to make her love him.

The past, though, could get in the way. He had lovers in his history—they both did—some experienced, some not, but there was always sweetness about them in the beginning. Shyness in bed.

Past lovers would undress in a bashful manner, hide beneath the sheets, watch what they said, how they breathed, how they made love, careful not to devolve into something visceral or animalistic. That wasn't Eloise Ann. From the opening night, she let him know how badly she needed him and what she would do to make him happy. At first it pleased him to no end. She was a revelation. In the heat of passion she could stop his heart, and, in the beginning, he used this as a reason to love her.

The pitcher understands how repetition trains the muscles. Eloise Ann knows all about repetition, too. He tries to forget, but it floods his mind when their bodies, slick with sweat, collapse on the bed. It's the only thing he can think about as he struggles to catch his breath.

——————

Jeremy Dove cried the night Frankie B told him he couldn't get an erection—deep, uncontrollable sobs locked away in the bathroom. He sat with his back turned and face in his hands, ignoring Eloise Ann's repeated taps on the door. She had never in her life seen a man of his size moved to tears. It was frightening in the way that a suspension bridge swaying in the wind is frightening and somewhat unbelievable at the same time.

After what seemed hours the lock unclicked, and she crawled inside to find the bathroom light off and the shag rug wound between his long legs and fingers. Closing the door softly, she guided the rug away from his hands, remembering the cloudy day she had seen a mother with an infant playing on the riverbank, the mother and child's feet collapsed in mud, the brown waves lapping their ankles, and the yellow infant lifejacket hugging the baby's pouched tummy and neck with the same level of solicitude Eloise Ann wanted to use when holding the pitcher that night. She pressed against him in the dark, and the idea of becoming a thing that could keep him afloat seemed more and more possible.

We don't know what happens, she heard him whisper into her hair. We don't know what happens after we die. What if it's nothing? What if we fade away and no longer exist?

———

The members of the pitcher's family were old St. Louis money. They lived on the middle upper class side of the river where manners and social pleasantries were taught like grammar and arithmetic. The men—his father and brother-in-laws—wore blazers and button shirts with slacks. His sisters dressed in muted tones and clutched designer purses, looking far less striking but far more refined than Eloise Ann who sat cross legged in her chair, smoothing the folds of her navy dress and thumbing blonde curls from her glowing forehead. She smiled politely at dinner and answered questions, but she seemed disengaged, tense. Every time the conversation drifted toward something meaningful, her eyes wandered to the far side of the room.

The pitcher tried to include her, to give some outward expression of their togetherness. He found every excuse to touch her. "Pass the butter, would you El?" and "We both love the city. It's not overwhelming like L.A. or Chicago. It seems like home." He tried more than once to grasp her hand beneath the table, but she slipped away.

At that point in the season the pitcher was eight and six and his earned run average was just over three and a half. It was a good year so far, and he was throwing like the number two starter the heavyset analysts on the radio claimed he could be. He won two to nothing when he was on. He facilitated the game when he didn't have his best stuff, gave up four through seven and allowed his team a puncher's chance.

The season took a turn during the worst part of the heat. The club started an eleven-day homestand. They dropped four of five, then six of seven. The players would remove their caps and dunk their heads in a cooler of ice and water between innings. The pitcher remembers squinting through the vapor into the stands, his feet baking in the dirt, his leather glove heavy with sweat. He remembers thinking: Is anybody even watching?

———

"Dove, I didn't think I'd see you again," said Frankie B. "Big-shot superstar doesn't want to visit the kiddies in the hospital with the burned up asses."

"I brought you something."

"Game ball. You brought me a game ball, didn't you?"

"No. It's something else. Something better. Are the nurses watching?"

He slipped a magazine, facedown, under Frankie B's good arm. The kid looked at the cover and threw the magazine on the floor.

"Screw you."

The pitcher picked the magazine up and flipped through it. "When I was thirteen, me and my cousins used to sneak into my uncle's camper. He had a huge stack, and we would look at em for hours. We had a rating system, one through ten: rack, ass, and face."

"So what?"

"This is a man's magazine. This is what we read. I think it's time you owned one, right?"

"Why would I want to own this magazine?"

"Don't you like tits?"

"Of course I like tits. But why would I need this?"

"If you don't want it, I'll take it back."

"Why would you give a kid who can't get a hard-on this stupid magazine?"

"One doctor says you can't get an erection. So what? Doctors don't know everything."

"Listen, dummy. My nerves got fried."

"They might regenerate."

"That doesn't happen."

"Says who?"

"Says the doctor for Christ's sake. What is it with this guy?"

"All your life people set your limits." The pitcher was on his feet and, for some reason, trying not to shout. "Are you going to let everybody say what you can and can't do? Everybody says you can't be happy. What are you going to tell them?"

"I don't know."

"Are you going to shit your bedpan and cry about it?"

"I said I don't know."

"Tell them you aren't going to stop trying. Tell them you want to look at the magazine."

————

The weeks moved on, but the sun refused. As the Major League Baseball trade deadline neared, Eloise Ann fantasized about sleeping with another man. It was all she could think about. She along with everyone else suffered from irritability and slight dehydration. The sun was stealing her happiness; it was stealing her water. She couldn't handle the pitcher's mood. He paced the bedroom in the middle of the night, waiting for the phone to ring. He followed Twitter incessantly and texted his teammates at all hours. He and Eloise Ann still made love every night, like clockwork desperation, but she found him intolerable. She needed him badly, but as soon as he rolled off, she wished he would breathe more quietly. She wished there was less hair on his arms. She wished he would stop trying to kiss her when it was over, leave her breasts alone for once. She wanted her fix, and then she wanted to go to sleep.

There were rumors, of course, the team being out of the race, that they would be sellers, and in-the-know analysts floated the pitcher's name as a trade possibility. He might retrieve a prospect or two. He might bring a needed bat. He had a team-friendly salary, and that made him marketable. A club on the coast was said to be salivating at seeing the pitcher in their uniform. Jeremy Dove couldn't handle the trade rumblings. It was like everybody talking behind your back and in front of your face at the same time. He couldn't leave. Not now.

One night he asked her, "What do you think of San Francisco?"

She didn't look up from her laptop. "I think it's a city in California with a big orange bridge."

"You don't really care about any of this, do you?"

"It doesn't involve me."

"Don't say that. This is our life."

"It's your life."

He got right in her face, then, his large hands grasping her shoulders. She realized how much bigger he was, like a giant, hurt and angry at the same time. "You talk this way when we fight. My dad used to say terrible things to my mom. My mom would say terrible things back. Even if you don't mean everything you say, people still listen. People remember."

"I don't know if I can come with you."

"That's a flat-out lie. You'd jump at the chance to leave this city. You'd beg me to take you."

"Don't pretend you know me. We're practically strangers."

"We're strangers now? I should be writing this down."

"You aren't the first guy to ask me to run away," she said. "I've turned down offers before. Better offers."

When she said it, she figured there was nothing else to say. The dam would break and everything would be over. And maybe that should have been the night their relationship ended, but it wasn't. A little after five in the morning, he woke to her standing above the couch. She was wearing one of his shirts, shivering uncontrollably, and it was all he could do to hold her up as she fell on him, kissing and crying and apologizing in the way that lovers do when they don't really want to think about whether what they are doing is right or wrong, they just can't stand the thought of not being near the other. And when they finally fell asleep on the floor next to the coffee table, they both felt that they had reached a new plateau, maybe, a new level of understanding. They both thought they had found exactly what they were looking for, and it was each other.

————

There was a small time they both remembered, maybe their best time. They had only known each other for a few days, and he had met her behind the coffee shop for a walk through the nightlife of downtown streets in search of a cold beer or margarita. The sunset had quelled the heat, at least for the early evening, and they moved through the city hand in hand, like couples do, talking about trivialities such as what it was like to be eighteen or twenty-two or twenty-six years old, or how their first self-cooked meal had tasted, or what it was like to fall asleep in a city where no one knows your name. After a while, Eloise Ann stopped noticing the pedestrian's stares, the guys in passing who lifted their cell phones or reached to shake the pitcher's hand. The buildings and streetlights fell into the backdrop and there was only him, the sidewalk, and the sensation of fingers interlaced with hers.

The patrons in a crowded bar on the edge of the Power and Light District recognized him immediately. Within seconds, the entire establishment rallied the call to bring the pitcher inside. Two hundred arms beckoned from the patio. They shouted his name from the balcony. College girls, dressed to the nines, blushed in his direction. The invitation rose to a crescendo as the couple pushed through the gathering throng.

Eloise Ann felt suddenly aware of the sweat gathering at the small of her back, the fadedness of her work khakis and polo, and the scent of her skin which was not unlike vanilla syrup and steamed milk. She tried to let go of his hand, but he refused.

"Listen, I don't want to go inside," he said.

"You might not have a choice," she said. "They aren't taking no for an answer."

"Come with me then."

"I shouldn't."

"You should."

She said, "I'm sorry. I'm not ready for all this. I thought I was."

"I know, I know. It's fine. You can go home if you want to. I'm just tired of being by myself. I thought maybe things were changing."

"Because of me?"

The pitcher nodded, and she glanced at the faces around them, the strangers urging them to come inside. She bit her lip, feeling slightly dizzy.

"I hate being alone, too," she said. "I really do. You don't know me, though. I'm easy to fall in love with. No one stays in love with me."

He took both her hands.

"I'm not like normal people," he said. "I never give up."

She looked to the ground and said in a voice he could barely hear, "I can be awful. And it's easy to crush me."

"I get crushed, too," he said, "but I never give up."

Despite the rumors, the pitcher didn't get traded, and the July heat continued into the early days of August, but the temperatures didn't have the same teeth. Frankie B was released from the hospital, and he sat in the dugout box seats with the other sick kids from the Children's Place who survived the hottest month of the year. His arm was wrapped in blue gauze and he wore his hat cocked to the side. Eloise Ann filled her usual seat, bare feet up on the chair in front of her, watching the pitcher toss warm-up bullets in a meaningless division game in the waning weeks of a meaningless season. He looked to see her, wiped sweat from his eyes, and then over to Frankie. His minor league coaches had tried to teach him to only see and hear a crowd, not individual pieces, but that was a skill he could never master.

What would Eloise Ann say if he asked her to marry him at the end of the season? What if he paid for Frankie's medical bills and college, and they all set up house in the city? He could play out the rest of his career, and then he could get on as a sports broadcaster for the local news, maybe even talk radio. Baseball could provide a life. Over time, a person could learn to survive this heat.

He remembered what one coach, his triple-A manager, had told him on the day of his rookie call-up. It had nothing to do with congratulations or here's what to expect. It wasn't "remember where you came from" or "put in a good word for your old skipper." His advice was all about the integrity of baseball, the legacy of the game. To a spectator who can only afford one live baseball game a year, the manager told him, it doesn't matter if a team is in first or last. Nothing matters except that one single game. He hoped the pitcher would never forget that.

The thing about the sun was you could hide from it. You could find shelter or shade. This was a pitcher's shade: the smattering of crowd on a Sunday afternoon; the loose banter of a team that was really just in it for the stats, the money, or the love of the game. He was in it for her, Eloise Ann, and the chance to do something that so few people were given an opportunity to do. He stared at her for a moment and thought this might be the last time he saw her in this way. Today she could be his prize—his to win. He could control whether or not she stayed. As long as he was here, bathed in the limelight, and she was there, a face in the crowd, she would never leave him.

When the first batter entered the box, the pitcher took a deep breath and stepped to the rubber as if his life depended on every throw.

STRAW MAN

The Mexicans at the jetty are stepping on black bass. The fish they catch do not meet regulation, so they stand on them, squeezing fin and scale between heel and rock, until the body extends. The fish transforms into a longer version of itself. *Flattened.* The woman is frantic as she explains this to me. I should arrest the Mexicans. I should prosecute. But I'm not a cop or a lawyer. The most I can do is call the police on my radio, but I don't do that either.

The woman's eyes fill with tears. She's early forties, glistening sweat through a plus-size pink cardigan. Like a nervous tic, her gaze flits back and forth between my face and the two boys with wheat-colored hair (her sons?) who yell and laugh as they play balance beam on the concrete dividers in the parking lot. I explain that a fish goes into shock when it comes out of water. Imagine if you ate a chicken sandwich, and an incredibly strong, invisible wire yanked you out of the atmosphere, into outer space. Think about how our sophisticated mind couldn't process that pain. Think about how stupid a fish brain is.

One of the boys says fuck you to his brother. He has fallen from the concrete divider, and a patch of blood stains his left knee. The woman flinches but makes no move to scold the children. Maybe they aren't hers after all. The hurt boy remains down for only a moment, then he remounts the divider, seemingly happy.

I turn my head to the shoulder radio. I call unit 4 to whoever is out there. Waterpatrol Craig comes back, and I ask if he will do a license check at the west side jetty. He says, ten-four. The woman seems satisfied by the official-sounding radio talk. Make sure and check the gills, she says. Mexicans stuff rocks in the gills.

———

Working for the DNR is my summer life. During the school year, I study graduate English at Central Iowa University—they even let me teach a section of freshman composition—but I spend May through August at the lake. This is my third year, and I've grown to like it. I ride a Dixie Chopper mower in the afternoon, and then patrol the grounds in the ranger's truck after four o' clock. Every now and then, I see disturbing things. A woman who hit her mouth on the windshield in a fender bender showed me a hornet's nest of cut lips and teeth. I shined a spotlight, once, on a naked couple in their fifties rolling in the sand and making animal noises. Another time I found a runner collapsed, face down, on the bike trail. I thought he was dead, but he had torn his ACL. It hurt too much to move.

My worst memory is of an old black fisherman. He waved my truck to his bench alongside the north Hampton bathroom. He had a thick mustache and strands of silver folded under a green Pioneer seed hat. His rock-hard belly ballooned into his lap. Did I hear the news, he wanted to know. I hadn't. "Young man," he said. "The end of this road is a terrible place."

I didn't understand what he meant, but the hair on the back of my neck stood and goose bumps peppered my forearms. The old man said I ought to turn around, he'd already phoned the police.

I expected the worst—a catastrophe beyond words. The reality was less exciting. A man in a pickup truck had shot himself in the cul-de-sac by the Inland Cat shelter. There wasn't anything dramatic like a blood covered windshield. He was just slumped, dead against the steering wheel. People say it looked like he passed out.

I never saw him, of course. When I told the old fisherman that it was my responsibility to drive to the end of the road, he stood in front of my truck with his hands on the hood. I was too young, he said. I was his son's age, and he would never let his son see a thing like he had seen. Wait for the police.

The first officer on duty, Chad, is eighteen months younger than me.

———

The fat lady with the kids (or whatever they are to her) asks if I will watch them while she goes to the bathroom. I don't know what she expects of me, but I agree. First I'm her cop, and now I'm her babysitter. She yells something about minding manners to the two boys with dirty blonde hair, and then waddles off to the port-a-potty.

Almost on cue, the kids appear in front of me, breathing hard. They want to show off. "I have a trick bike at home," says the older one. "It's a Dyno."

"That's good," I say.

"If you really want to be gay in school," he continues, "you ride a Huffy."

The little brother bristles. "You're gay," he says.

This starts a momentary wrestling match, or something close to it. They lock wrist to wrist and attempt to kick each other's ankles. Probably a year or two separates them in age, but they appear to be the exact same strength. "Listen," I say, "I used to have a BMX, but I broke the handlebars jumping a ramp. I'll show you the scar."

"We do jumps all the time," the younger one says, no longer interested in fighting. "I could maybe jump over a car."

"I could jump a semi-truck," says the older.

I'm starting to wonder what is keeping their mother. I ask them how long they expect her to be.

The older one laughs. "That's Aunt Hen. She's so fat. We could jump her fat belly, but I think it would be impossible. She eats all the time."

The younger goes into hysterics. "Aunt Hen is probably trying to poop all that food."

Both children squawk crazy with laughter. Then they resume

63

trying to kick each other in the ankle. They argue over which one is more gay. For a minute I feel that this woman has left me with these brats. Maybe she doubled back through the woods, and there was some big biker dude with a fantastic beard waiting to take her away.

It isn't too much longer before Aunt Hen emerges from the port-a-potty, her cheeks sunburned, her hair mussed. "Thank you so much," she says. "Did they sass you?"

"Absolutely."

—————

I don't know what I did to deserve Travis. He is waiting for me at the shop, smiling in ragged jeans and cutoff Led Zeppelin t-shirt. He's short, with bleached hair and teeth that sometimes don't touch and sometimes overlap, skinny, a chin that juts out like he's being pulled by an invisible beard. He has one long eyebrow in the shape of an M. A boy like him exists in every American sophomore class, one who takes no greater joy from life other than cutting some-body with a cruel word or sharp joke. Teeth and talons. He'd accuse Aunt Hen of stealing food meant for orphans, or maybe even eating one of the orphans if she were hungry enough. Those two brat kids would worship the ground on which he walks.

If Travis speaks, he lies. He brags about what it smells like be-tween the legs of girls in his high school. When I'm driving him around in the truck, he holds his fingers to his face and inhales. Then he offers me the scent of his hand. The other DNR guys have various Travis nicknames: Virgin, The Jew, Nutjob, Needledick. As he's explained to me, black guys, especially the one dating his sis-ter, never leave the couch unless it's out to the mailbox to retrieve the check Obama sent. Don't get him started on rappers, either. They make decent music, sure, but he can't stand the way they talk—crunk this, crunk that—and he hates how they cruise around in their bright purple cars with the windows down, and those ri-diculous, oversized spinning rims.

Two hundred hours of community service in six weeks. That's

what he owes. Waterpatrol Craig thinks Travis got caught with a whole bunch of Ecstasy, or busted in a school parking lot selling marijuana. Though technically a criminal, Travis isn't scary like some parolees under the DNR's watch. The thirty-something with huge, fat forearms, as an example, beat his next door neighbor within an inch of life. Fat-arms doesn't talk to you when you drive him around, just stares out the window, stewing pestilence. We also have one high school civics teacher who tries to pass her community service off as charity. She pays restitution for her DUI by picking up diapers and cigarette butts on the beach. A hat and broad sunglasses cover her face. She'd wear a mask, probably, if they'd let her.

It occurred to me a couple days ago that Travis likes me. I'm the youngest one of the crew, and really, the only one he talks to. For all intents and purposes, I am the surrogate older brother of a juvenile offender. I don't know how I feel about that.

"They sent me home," he says. He's referring to his landscaping job. "I broke a weedeater."

He climbs in the truck and immediately turns on rap music, the only station we ever listen to.

I drop Travis off on the dam with trash tweezers and a big sack.

"This takes at least an hour," I say. "Go down the shoreline. Pick up all the garbage. Don't slip and bust your brains on the rocks."

"Aye, aye, Cap'n."

"Try not to spend the whole hour jerking off," I add. I don't know why I say it, but the kid smiles. I shouldn't joke with him.

By the time I drive the truck halfway down the road, Travis is sitting on the riprap talking on his cell phone. As usual, he isn't going to do a goddamn thing . After work and on his days off, he comes by and pretends to sweep or shovel or mow, and Sutton, the manager, signs his community service sheet. Sutton feels a duty to punish parolees. He assigns them awful tasks: organizing cans in the pole shed known as WaspLand USA, or running a push-mower along the disc golf fairways where poison ivy leaves out-number blades of grass. Travis is afraid of Sutton. Sutton could call the parole officer. The parole officer could call the judge.

———

Waterpatrol Craig is waiting for me at the beach. Of all the black people I know, he's the only one who wants to be a country boy. Travis says he's the lone gang banger on the block drinking a forty-ounce bottle of Pabst. He wears aviator sunglasses over his dark-skinned face; a Velcro, policeman belt holds his radio and flash-light. He likes chewing tobacco, big trucks, and farm girls in tight blue jeans. His lifelong dream is to join the ranks of the conserva-tion officers—the biggest and baddest soldiers in the DNR army, who spend their year chasing whitetail poachers all over the state.

"Guys at the jetty had a couple expired licenses," he says. "Wrote em up."

I tell him about Aunt Hen and the mutilated fish.

"Heard they do that, but these Mexicans here no speak-y Eng-lish," Craig says.

He spits Copenhagen juice, and then continues, "I take it you're stuck with the little drug addict. Kid's been stealing beer out of the confiscation fridge. Watch him close. If you catch the little fucker, call the cops. He's violating parole."

I nod, and we both stare out at the small crowd populating the sand—ninety people, maybe a hundred. Part of me really doesn't like Craig. The look in his eyes tells me that he will make the worst kind of officer: one who enjoys ordering people to lower their voices. It thrills him when the sight of his uniform catches a man's breath, when that man willingly allows him a look inside a locked door, a glove box, or a livewell. Nothing in the world could excite Craig more than the thought of asking a woman to prove she has nothing to hide underneath her clothes. The secret doesn't mat-ter. What gets him off is turning the key. Law Enforcement majors in my classes are the same. Even before they serve a day on the force, they act like they've joined a brotherhood of sacrifice and privilege. They look at me with smug satisfaction, knowing that they're the ones I'll be calling if I hear the front door creak open in the middle of the night. I'll come running right to them.

But there are other times when Craig acts with more humanity. He and I participated, once, in the rescue of an injured horse. The owner, a hard-faced woman with rough skin and thick, braided hair, drove me around the park looking for her lost filly. She lived on a small hobby-farm several miles away, and though she was certain the filly was gone forever, she kept her eyes glued to the pastures on either side of the road. We spotted the horse standing at the edge of the woods between the fishermen's trail and Atlantic Shelter. I don't know if I've seen a sadder sight. The filly had broken its neck a month before she ran away. She still retained the ability to walk, run even, but she was hobbled by substantial nerve damage. She shook terribly, as if punch drunk by late-stage Parkinson's. Her neck curved in an unnatural way, causing her head to hang in crippled obedience. You could see the muscles inexorably twitch, her eyes water.

Waterpatrol Craig had already found her, and he was talking to the horse gently when we arrived at the scene. He stroked her snout, and she eased into his hand, like an oversized dog seeking affection. "It's alright," he said to her. "Everything's going to be okay." The filly, when she saw me, cowered in fear. She backpedaled in an effort to hide behind Craig. I couldn't take another step. To think that horse was in such pain that the simple presence of a human face was enough to shame it into retreat.

Craig talked in a different tone, then, when he helped the filly's owner load her stock into the trailer. "Promise you won't give up on her," he said, placing his hand on the woman's sleeve. "She wants so badly to stay alive. "

———

Thirty minutes later, I check on Travis. The dam is empty, but I spot him two football fields down the shoreline hiding by a willow tree. In the sun's glare, he appears as a shadow perched at the water's edge. The lake continues to the northwest through the Lost Lake access channel, but the land we maintain ends here. There's a yellow stake driven into the earth twenty yards past where he sits on the riprap, texting. That's the DNR property boundary. If he were to get up and saunter ten steps to the left, he would no longer be my problem. On my way over, I pass a crumpled bag and the trash tweezers wedged between two rocks.

"You done already?"

"I can't go on," he says, not looking up from his phone. "I'm too thirsty."

"There's a lake right there to drink from."

He doesn't respond, shakes his head and grins at the buzzing phone before clicking more buttons.

"Who are you talking to?"

"This girl, you don't know her," he says. "You wish you knew her, though. Tits like buttercream, unbelievable."

I stand there, stupidly, hoping he will rise and start picking up trash, but he makes no effort to move from the rocks. August is nearly finished, but summer remains in full force, and my hand is slick with sweat after wiping my forehead. I take off my sunglasses, and clean the lenses on my uniform.

"Be back in a half hour," I say, finally, "Bossman should be rolling through any minute in the ranger truck."

"Okay," he says. "Grab me a Gatorade from the marina. I'll owe you a dollar."

———

It's funny how an unremarkable time sticks to memory. I remember riding in the back of a pickup truck: warm sun on my bare forearms; the rumble of a neglected muffler; the smell of cut, yellowed grass. We had just dumped a load of tree clippings by the 100th Street boat ramp, and it was a long, twenty-five mile an hour drive to retrieve the mowers at the beach.

It was odd to me, laying my head against the lip of the bed, that I could enjoy the back of a pickup truck, floating along, no choices to make, no responsibility to own. My troubles consisted of waiting out a shift's end, my itching legs, the uncomfortable shell of sunscreen dried to my face. That was me. And then there was the guy who shot himself by the Inland Cat shelter two months earlier. He sat in the front seat. At twenty-four years old, I didn't take much seriously. I didn't try to rationalize concepts like death, aging, or even fatherhood. Lack of responsibility felt safe. What would I say, for instance, when one day explaining to my children how a man could place a gun barrel inside his mouth? Would I bend the truth—tell them how the man suffered from a terminal illness, or that he couldn't live with the guilt of hitting his wife in the face with a broken bottle?

Maybe I would say that the man couldn't handle riding anymore. He wanted to drive, to feel the steering wheel between his knuckles and the rotation of tires responding to his every move. Bad choices became so real, I'd say, he could see them beckoning him forward like ghosts on the windshield.

But how could he do it? They'd want to know. How could he give away the only thing worth protecting?

You have to dare yourself, sweethearts. Don't think about the aftermath. Just pull. But promise me you'll never do that, no matter how much it hurts. Find me, first.

I want so badly to save you.

———

I walk the beach. Show some newlyweds how to keep their Alaskan Husky cool. Give directions to an old guy. A couple girls in yellow bikinis ask if they can bring liquor on the sand. As long as it's in a plastic cup, I don't care. An hour passes, maybe ninety minutes. The sun is high overhead before I remember to retrieve Travis.

When I hurry back to the dam, I don't like what I see. Waterpatrol Craig and Earl, another summer employee, are messing with him from the DNR boat. They have him wading in the water after a floating life jacket. It's a faded bubble of orange, half sunk, twenty feet from shore. Travis doesn't know what is going to happen. Fif-

69

teen feet north of the riprap, he'll step off a cliff. The water will go from his knees to well over his head. I've watched fishermen do it. They wade out in the warm mud only to find themselves plunging like a lead weight into an ocean of cold water.

By the time I remove the buzzing key from the truck ignition, I've already heard the yell. Travis has stepped into Craig and Earl's trap. He flounders in the dirty water. For a moment, he disappears. Then he resurfaces, gagging and coughing. He bobs up and down several times, a yellow bonnet of bleached hair plastered to his head. Finally, he snares the wasted life jacket and hugs it to his chest. In the boat, Waterpatrol Craig and Earl have a total cow.

"Fuck you," Travis says, "I can't swim."

I can hear his breathing from shore—short, uncontrolled bursts. He clings to the life jacket. I think he's crying, or trying very hard not to.

"Kick your legs," I say. "You don't have to swim. Three or four kicks and you're in the shallows."

I worry for a second that I will have to wade in after him, but he buries his yellow head into the blaze orange pillow and frogkicks toward shore.

"You okay?" I ask when he pulls himself onto the riprap.

"You're dead," he says. I imagine he's talking to the guys in the boat, but his back is turned. He marches down the shoreline to where he left his shoes and cell phone. He steps into his sneakers, then chucks the garbage bag and trash tweezers as far as he can into the lake. The bag floats, but the tweezers instantly sink and are gone. I don't think they are expensive, but I know what Craig will do even before he does it.

"Get Sutton on the radio," he says to Earl. He's no longer laughing. "This kid's going to prison."

"Take it easy," I say. "He couldn't swim."

I'm not ready for what happens next. From my vantage Travis bends over to tie his shoelaces, but he rises up with a handful of stones. Before I can say another word, the air is full of them. I see them floating in slow motion, lazy arcs over the water. The rocks make one or two backward rotations. I know right where they are going to land. I wish for one crazy moment that he threw them at me.

The guys had dropped anchor maybe thirty feet from shore. The first stone grazes Earl's shoulder. The next one dings the hull. A third puts a ten-inch spiderweb in the glass windscreen. It's not the worst thing a guy could do. It's not as if Travis pulled a semi-automatic weapon and unloaded it at them, but that is how Waterpatrol Craig reacts. He yells at the top of his lungs, and I'm sure he's using his cop lingo—assault and parole officer and felony and I don't know what. Travis reloads, barks back, and hurls more rocks. Earl guns the motor, trying to retreat to deep water, but the old outboard sputters and stalls. Earl says goddamnit and pulls hard on the cord. Travis throws more rocks. An older couple shore-fishing on the west bank hurries to reel in their lines. The seagulls hanging out on the dam go absolutely berserk.

I don't hear any of it, not really. None of it registers. I crouch in the grass, eyes closed, hands pressed against the sides of my head —probably some reflex I never knew I had. Warmth fills my chest, spreading to my shoulders, eyebrows, and ears. My knees quiver.

I'm trying to figure out why any of this is happening. How did I end up here, on the edge of a lake, stuck between a rock fight and a hard place? It doesn't help that Craig is black, and Travis spends all day hating on black people. It doesn't help that Craig would call the police on his firstborn son, or that Travis can't swim, or that I should have been back to get him thirty minutes ago. I don't care who's to blame. I just want it to be a month from now—it's mid-September and I'm back in the classroom. All of this seems like another life or another place. Travis is just a story. Craig is a device, and I am a metaphor.

When I look up, the moment has passed. The patrol boat has retreated to the far shore, and the seagulls have calmed. The old couple's lines are back in the water. Travis has a strange expression on his face, and it takes a moment to realize what he's staring at.

It's me.

———

The road between the dam and the shop isn't two miles, but it feels like the longest highway in the Central Plains. Travis buzzes like a disturbed hornet. He unbuckles and re-buckles his seatbelt, rolls down the window, spits, and then rolls it up. Over and over, he talks me through the scenario, the way it all went down. He wants to know if I am on his side.

"He's going to bury me, isn't he?" he says. He's talking about Sutton. "I can't be responsible for fighting back. They almost drowned me."

"I don't know what he's going to say."

"You were there. Tell 'em what happened."

"I don't know what he's going to say," I repeat. I do, though. I know exactly. Sutton doesn't put up with nonsense. He'll call the parole officer this afternoon.

Travis balls his fist. He cusses and pounds the dash. "Those guys said my mom can't afford groceries. She goes around sucking dicks for foodstamps."

He's lying again. I say, "Why were they making you get the life-jacket?"

"Because."

"Don't mess around. Because why?"

"Because they said a couple beers magically disappeared from the fridge."

"Did you take them?"

Travis doesn't answer.

"I can't believe you took that beer. It's expired. We pick that stuff up from minors at the beach."

Travis looks out the window. His fingers flicker to the door handle, tap it lightly, then the window crank, and finally the lock bolt. He presses the bolt, but changes his mind and tries to pincer it back up. The lock won't budge. "It doesn't matter if I took the beer," he says.

I expect him to say more, but he, instead, picks up the sweating Gatorade in the cup holder between us, cracks it, and drinks deeply. After what seems like a never-ending drink, he wipes his mouth, breathing hard.

"I owe you a buck," he says, and then, almost like an after-thought, "Goddamn, check out that fatty."

I look to see where he's pointing. Coming up on the right side of the road, there's a large, shoulder-hunched woman plodding through the grass toward a parked station wagon. She's walking with a lawn chair tucked under an arm. I recognize her immediately: Aunt Hen. The two brats with shaggy, wheat-colored hair are not far behind, careening back and forth like inner-tubes hitched to a mammoth pontoon boat.

I ease off the gas and raise a hand in greeting. Aunt Hen doesn't notice. Clearly, the last several hours have drained all the perspiration from her body and the redness from her face. Her eyes stay forward, her steps purposeful. She doesn't acknowledge her two trailing burdens. Their day at the lake is over. She's on a mission: keys already out, one foot in front of the other. Nothing in the world can stand between her and the station wagon. The two boys are a different story. Both have melon-slice grins plastered to their faces. One is doing an impression of fat, old Aunt Hen, lumbering forth with puffed cheeks. His sleeves hang limp and armless. His hidden hands balloon a huge belly out of his shirt. Each bumbling step causes the younger brother to twist and contort with laughter.

I give the boys a quick honk from the DNR truck, and they lose their minds. They bounce up and down and wave furiously—hummingbirds gorged on Mexican jumping beans. For a moment, I'm forgetting about everything. I'm shaking my head and smiling. Stupid little fuckers.

Travis stares at me like I've gone crazy. He turns around in his seat and checks through the back window.

"They're flipping us off," he announces. He sounds almost happy when he says it.

73

THE TENTH HIGHEST
MOUNTAIN IN THE WORLD

There I am in my car with my fingers fluttering against the keys in the ignition. My blue striped tie hangs between my knees. The windows are stiff with ice, and the lights from the church glow like candles in the rear-view mirror.

Last night I had a dream, again, about the summit brink of Cerro Torre in Argentina. My therapist refers to this condition I have as "nocturnal acrophobia" which means I dream about being stuck in environments where I am higher than my sense of equilibrium wants me to be. I always have nightmares about Cerro Torre. People should have never been allowed to take pictures of it, let alone climb it. My dream starts with miles and miles of cirrus clouds, close enough to touch. A strong gust of wind. Then I am clinging to the North face—nothing between me and the ground but a mile high spike of brown granite. Another gust and I'm sliding down the vertical stone, my fingers leaving ten bloody trails. I close my eyes right before my body hits the glacier cellar. The next thing I know, I'm tearing the sheets off my bed, sitting up and wondering: would it hurt or would I just be dead?

———

My best friend David is half-American, half-Syrian. Today, his afternoon wedding started twenty minutes late. Before the ceremony, his little brother Hector spilled booze down the front of his tuxedo, postponing the two o' clock start until Hector could be screamed at and cleaned off. I sat on the groom's side, six pews from the front. My mom sat on my left, my dad on my right.

Jesus Christ was very large at David's wedding. In the stained-glass window, Christ's massive likeness loomed overhead. We were a boxful of mice staring up at the big cat. They used tan glass for the skin, white for the robe. David looked tiny, waiting in his black tuxedo underneath Jesus. I waved to him, but he didn't see me.

There must still be some traces of puberty left in my body. All I could think about as the music started and Holly sobbed her way down the aisle was her and David consummating their marriage on a stiff hotel bed. While everyone else whispered things like: "I love that dress" and "there's an angel in this room," I thought about David and Holly having awkward virgin sex.

It was a small wedding party. David and his brother, grinning like a kid caught with his hand in the cookie jar, and Holly and her older sister. A couple weeks ago, while we were swimming laps in the rec center, David mentioned the purposelessness of grooms-men. When I popped my head out of the water between laps thir-teen and fourteen he scrunched his face and said, "They just stand there, you know. Not really necessary."

I took a step back and let the water rise up to where my mus-tache would have been.

"I would have picked you as one of them, though," he said. "Groomsmen, I mean. I made a couple lists, but I couldn't get it below eight guys. That's too many."

I told him I understood, but I didn't really. I thought there was a purpose. I still do.

———

At the reception, I sat in my assigned seat and drank non-alcohol-ic punch from a Dixie cup. My dad leaned over and said that he'd never been to a wedding before where he couldn't get a beer. I swallowed what was left in the Dixie cup, wishing for the burn of a shot, but tasted only sweet. Stupid, sweet non-alcoholic punch.

Then my mom tapped a finger on the table and said, hey, that's Cindy Hughes over there. That's when everything started to get fuzzy. Things started to go wrong. It was like all the blood vessels in my face filled at once. High school came back in seconds, and my head turned into a cooked tomato. Cindy Hughes was sitting at the next table, sucking on the tip of her spoon and leaning forward, ever so slightly. Breasts. She had them. Huge, gigantic, pillow breasts. The type of breasts that people develop crushes on. And I, of course, did have a crush, not so much on her—though I thought she was pretty cool—but more on everything hidden underneath her sleeveless black dress. High school was definitely coming back: wet dreams, the volleyball girls' damp hair, sleepovers where David and I discussed, in detail, all the females in our class we wanted to date or just have one earth-shattering night of sex with. Cindy Hughes was sitting less than fifteen feet away. And she had made my list every single time.

My therapist and I once had a long conversation about Cindy Hughes' breasts. We decided they were something I was incredibly drawn to and afraid of at the same time. He called it a "paradoxical desire."

My mom said that Cindy had been looking at me. She said that I had to ask Cindy to dance later, or she would make my dad do it for me. I told her that Cindy surely had a boyfriend, but my mom said that everybody (and by everybody she meant all normal people in the world) who has a special someone to bring to a wedding, brings them. People would rather not go than go stag.

"Okay, Christ, I get it," I said. I stood up from my chair.

I waved and stepped over to Cindy. She met me with a friendly, hips-back hug that pressed our chests together. As her giant breasts flattened against me, my eyes closed and there I was again on Cerro Torre, hanging on against the screaming Argentinean wind. When she let go, I felt myself start to fall. The only thing left of me was ten red finger-trails on brown granite.

———

Sometimes I have good dreams, too. The girl I want to marry is Annapurna I, the tenth highest mountain in the world. Everyone else is afraid of her katabatic winds, her avalanches that come without warning, her ice shelves that break away and swallow mountaineers with outstretched arms. When I get my chance, I'll drag my way up, inch by inch through stripes of ruddy stone, shadow, and ice, until I see snowlight and blue sky swirling above like a Van Gogh painting. Everyone else wants to look at Lhotse. They look at Broad Peak and K2, voluptuous and picturesque like the silhouettes of blonde bombshells. They don't see the simple beauty, the powder of Annapurna's wind-touched cheeks. They don't know what it's like to stand with popped ears, all alone, in her summit's blinding light. All they want is to climb up and get down.

On the crest of Annapurna, sun shines and shines. If I make it to the top, I'm never coming down.

———

When Hector saw me sitting with Cindy, he pulled away from his relatives and waved furiously for me to come talk.

"You bet your white ass I'm drunk again," he said. "I just met half my family and, wouldn't you know, they're all Muslims."

"Yeah, so?"

"It's against their religion, you dense motherfucker," he said, slapping my arm. "That's why we can't have booze out in public."

"I know that."

"David and Holly, man," he said. He steadied himself against me. "They're on the top of the mountain. No, scratch that, the top of the world. They made it, you know? And I'm proud as shit."

I clenched my fists. For some reason, the word "mountain" coming out of Hector's mouth made me want to knock his face in. He couldn't mean anything by it. Aside from my therapist, I've never told anyone about my nightmares, not even David, but the simple sound of the word struck a nerve. I wouldn't say this about most people, but Hector has the type of face that you want to punch from time to time. He has a bulb nose, and his chin sticks out at a funny angle. He has little, darting eyes and puffed cheeks. It's like he wants you to hit him—like his face is just a piece of meat that will work itself back to normal no matter how many times you beat against it.

"Why are you looking at me that way?" said Hector. He coughed and grabbed my tie. "Christ, the least you can do is go out behind the church and drink shots with me."

——

Edmund Hillary and Tenzing Norgay have always claimed that they summitted Mount Everest simultaneously. But I have often wondered if Hillary, while descending the razor thin ridge to the Southern peak, had thought, for one hypoxic moment, about sticking his crampon in Tenzing's back and giving him a nice little shove and "fuck you, Sherpa" right off the edge into hell. Maybe he couldn't take the thought of his Himalayan friend being brained by a giant ice boulder or sucked into a crevasse like an insect pressed up in a tissue. Or maybe, since it was such a long fall, he didn't want to listen to all the things Tenzing would be able to scream on the way down, things like: "I carried your fat, bee-keeping ass to the top" or "You'll wish I was there to make you magic tea when you freeze to death in your fucking tent. "

Then again, Hillary may have just decided to share and wouldn't have considered any of those other alternatives. Some people aren't selfish. Part of me, though, believes he at least thought about it.

I spent the 150 dollars I had saved for a tuxedo replacing the starter in my Toyota. Hector spent 150 dollars on booze and decided that I was one dense motherfucker.

——

When the best man and I came back inside, the party had turned from American social hour to international dance party. David's relatives, flown in from overseas, had located the DJ and given him some of their world-beat CDs. Foreign instruments and Arabic thumped out of the speakers. His relatives slapped their hands together. They formed a large circle in the middle of the dance floor.

Mustached uncles and cousins lifted the bride and groom onto their shoulders. The noise level continued to rise as they bounced the couple around the room. Holly screamed. David laughed as if it were the most normal thing in the world.

My mom and dad stood up, but they didn't leave the table. They clapped along as the relatives carried David and his bride around the dance floor. Over the music, my mom said that this was great, and we should do things like this at our own weddings. When my mom says "our," she means white people.

I felt a tug at my sleeve. There was Cindy Hughes, smiling and pulling me toward the middle of the dance floor. I was drunk. Her huge breasts beckoned to me from under her bra. I wanted to touch them, suckle them, talk to them even. I wanted to lead her outside, remove that dress, and take her in the snow as if we were making love to each other on the mushroom icecap that guards the summit tip of Cerro Torre.

She pulled my tie until my ear met her lips and told me that she felt obligated, since she didn't have a date, to at least have a dance partner if she was going out on the floor. I tried to tell her I couldn't dance, but she towed me into the mass of clapping Arabs.

David was somewhere in the center of the crowd, but I couldn't see him. I wished I was standing next to him, in a tuxedo with Cindy Hughes as my date, and he was laughing and putting his arm around my shoulders and telling all his relatives what a great and funny guy I was, how I always pushed him to swim harder and faster at the pool, how I had chipped in financial aid to bail his brother out of a DUI, how I always showed up when he needed somebody to talk to or go to the bar with, and, if there's one person he thought absolutely had to be there to support him on the day of his wedding, that person was me. But he was right in the middle of everything, and I was on the fringe.

Cindy Hughes took my wrists and made me clap along with the rest of the crowd. I raised my arms and moved closer. She smiled.

Something hit me hard in the back, and the next thing I knew, I was face down on the dance floor's wooden tiles. The uncles, carrying David again, did not realize they had knocked me over. The party continued above my shoulders. As people stepped around me, I could see shining loafers and wingtips, landing and rising inches from my face.

———

It was this moment—me strung out all over the dance floor—that my therapist will point to as the "skeleton key of anxiety," because, when I was lying there, I didn't feel like I needed to get up. Sure, someone could have stepped on my head or my balls, and Cindy Hughes must have had some sort of reaction, but neither of those reasons seemed important enough to pull myself off the floor.

That moment was all about me and my problems, and the fact that nobody gave a shit that I was down there, beneath all those feet, waiting to be stomped.

———

So, now I'm right here, strapped in my Toyota by myself. I want to start my car and let the warmth flow through the dash, but I can't figure out how to make my fingers move.

Or maybe I'm actually asleep. And maybe I'm not in my car, but sitting with my head down on top of Vinson Massif—the tallest dune in Antarctica's frozen desert. There's nothing around me. Only sundogs, diamond dust, and miles and miles of ice in every direction. No moss, no lichens, not even the toughest penguins or seals. Constant sun. Rainless clouds. Wind that never rests. Nothing alive wants to breathe the air on the bottom of the world.

Maybe this is where I'm supposed to be, stuck here in the cold. Maybe this is my new worst nightmare.

I'd like to think that's not the real me, though, sitting in the car, sitting on the mountaintop. I'd like to think the real me is inside the church, standing in the middle of the dance floor with his head

80

back, arms stretched out, eyes fixed on the hundreds of shadows moving against the ceiling lights. The real me is in motion. He spins and spins, opens and closes his eyes. One second, blankness. The next, he is one of the shadows, dancing in slow circles across the ceiling's white stage.

COLD TOWN

There was a monster in the woods, up on the hill. Jonas couldn't see him, not yet, but the monster was walking through a labyrinth of twenty-foot elm trees, lost in the buzz of the forest.

Jonas had run east out of Cold Town through Bard Owl Park and the south trailhead. He had already eclipsed the abandoned three-story house with strips of ashen paint scratched and hanging like wilted sepals. Legs fresh, breath steady, he was running at a seven-minute-and-fifteen-second clip—a pace he hoped he could keep when he ran the Twin Cities Half Marathon later that month. He was thirty-one years old with thick hair and a brow line that only receded when he pulled his bangs back. The October trees had just begun their slow turn, and the air tasted like wet leaves. A few had blown from their perch and lay crumpled on the bike path. Most remained firmly attached with streaks of yellow, brown and red—still alive but not yet showing full color.

The morning chill made Jonas opt for sleeves, shorts, his good race shoes, and iPod. In his thirties, he was tougher than he'd been in his twenties. The training bug had taken him by the throat about eighteen months ago, and now he could run forever. He could grasp the branch of a jungle gym or swing-set and pull his chin over the top of it fifteen times. He could do sixty push-ups without rest. In his twenties he was never competitive, but now that he had leveled up in age class, he was in a whole new playing field.

In the third quarter of mile two, he passed a cute girl in running tights. The curve of her thighs and backside shifted and contracted beneath the sheer black as she jogged steadily through the thickening woodland. He tightened his arms and abdomen as he overtook her on the left, hoping that she might, too, give him a stare as he glided past. Ten miles from now, none of this would matter. His muscles would be drained, and the only thing he would be able to rationalize was placing one foot in front of the next.

———

When Gwen and Jonas moved to Cold Town, it was by necessity, not choice. A little over three years ago Jonas had spread a map on the kitchen counter and put his finger on the name written sideways across the yellow line that marked highway 3.

You work here, he said moving his finger. I work here. I'll drive for an hour. You can drive for thirty minutes. That's how we'll get through.

Gwen bit her lip and bent over the counter for a closer look. Jonas could tell she didn't want the conversation, let alone the compromise. She never pictured them living in "the sticks," as she called it, but she desperately longed for a baby, and she didn't argue.

After Jonas put his finger on the map, things begin to fall into place faster than either of them expected. Jonas blinked and they were in escrow on their first house, a little split foyer on the north side of town. He blinked again, and he was wheeling his ten-speed up the ramp of the Budget truck—the last item to be loaded before closing the door. One final blink, and he was feeling Gwen's knees squeeze around his leg on their first night in the new house.

I think I'm ovulating, she said, swimming her hand up his shirt.

She reached beneath the thick quilts. When she wrapped her knees around him a second time, he could feel a dense tangle of hair against his leg, a gentle rocking. He could sense her hand stroking his stomach, searching below the elastic of his underwear.

Jonas looked toward the hallway. There's something outside, he said. I heard a noise.

What sort of noise?

Something, he said, leaning his head back. Babe, stop. This doesn't feel right.

You're not putting on a condom.

It's not that, he said. Those trains. What if there are drifters on those trains, and they knock on doors in the middle of the night. What are we going to do then? Does this town even have police?

We don't answer the door, she said.

They'll still be out there.

Gwen sat up, wincing as if listening for a faraway sound. She took his hand.

There's nothing outside, she said. I'm in here. What are you going to do about me?

———

Gunshot. Unmistakable in timbre and echo. Mile six and halfway up the Lamm's Canyon ascent, Jonas heard it, and immediately swiped away his headphones. He froze.

A runner doesn't imagine himself in crosshairs. He doesn't frighten himself with the image of a gun-barrel aimed at his face. Runners have other, more specific worries: the catastrophic misstep, cold sweats in the middle of heat, unraveling ankle ligaments, exercise induced angina that doesn't end when a runner slows to a stop and only gets worse when a runner sits on the concrete with a hand over the chest. More fears: the question mark of a copperhead snake darting out from a pile of leaves; a treed mountain lion pouncing from above; more likely, a pack of stray dogs.

A gunshot in the canyon was rare, but certainly plausible, certainly something to fear. A seasoned outdoorsman would ask: Where was it coming from? A hunter? A poacher? Were they mistaking me for game? Should I move? Should I yell? Should I make myself invisible?

Runner here, Jonas called out, his eyes scanning the hillcrest for the source of the noise. There was movement to the north. He could see the shape of a person stepping through the trees, a

84

man of medium height and build, maybe fifty yards away. Scraggly beard, faded green jacket, black baseball cap. He held a rifle in his hands.

There was something crawling below the man on the hill, something alive and wounded. The weeds near the edge of the trail were collapsed and quivering. What was trying to come out, though? Arms and legs? The spillage of long hair? Whatever was hurt continued to rustle as the man with the rifle stood over the top.

Jonas heard a noise come from the figure on the ground that was not unlike a gasp, but more of a warble, a choking sound, perhaps, but then the sound became clearer—like the wail of a tornado siren finally reaching you. At first you think it is the wind, but, no. It's danger, real and in your face. Pay attention, it says. Something's coming to get you.

As soon as Jonas heard the sound, he knew exactly what was happening. The wounded thing on the ground was a person, and that person was screaming.

The man with the rifle shot a second time, and the person on the ground didn't make any more noise. Jonas couldn't process. He couldn't move. Half a heartbeat, maybe. Another heartbeat, and then his instincts took over. Murderer, Jonas' mind sang. Murderer—like a klaxon, like a thousand little kids ratting out a killer in the playground. There. *Murderer*. Right in front of you. It's a murderer.

He wanted to point and yell it himself. Look what you did, he wanted to say. You shot somebody. You shot somebody twice, and you did it on purpose.

But Jonas couldn't talk because he could see, quite clearly, that the murderer was staring directly at him.

———

Earlier that summer Jonas walked along the trail through another portion of the same woods with his son Eddie strapped to his back. He hadn't used the words *dizzying chasm* before, but when he looked below the bridge at the bluff ravine that seemed to swallow all the foliage like some monstrous throat, no other expression could describe it. There was a stream down there, 150 feet below his ankles, and the stuffed dog—the dog his son had called Mr. Spots since he was able to form words—was prostrate on the creek bank.

The dog's not dead, he thought. It was never alive.

He had been taking Eddie to the trails for years, at first when the child was an infant belted to his dad's chest, and now as a mop-headed toddler who could walk on his own but preferred the comfort of his father's curved back and shoulder blades, the ability to wrap his easy arms around his father's neck when the terrain became too much.

Gwen, Jonas said into his cell phone. Eddie threw Spots off a cliff.

He could hear his wife inhale sharply, and then a few beats of silence. What are you going to do? she said.

I don't know.

You have to get it, she said.

That's not really possible.

You have to, she said. Do you hear what I'm saying? You have to.

––––

Gwen would complain of train whistles at night when they first moved to Cold Town, but, over time, Jonas would be surprised if he or she could sleep without the distant, hourly wails—the faraway friction of wheels on rail. The trains grew familiar, just like the town, the four hour thunderstorms that would come frantically once a week during summer, and the snows that would blanket the region between late October and April. Soon, setting and place and routine felt like home.

Cold Town, a survivor of violence, was founded in 1859 after the Sioux Indian Chief Sleepy Eye signed the Treaty of Traverse, which ceded control of many Sioux lands to the white settlers. Several outposts in the region were created as pioneers moved into what they thought would be comfortable locations to hunt and cultivate, and possible rail line stops in the aftermath of the industrial revolution. Many of the smaller townships disbanded after white blood was shed in the Spirit Lake Massacre, and even more after the Sioux uprising of 1862, but Cold Town lived on, and the population grew to sustainability by the turn of the century.

The Cold Town of today contains one of the last, true city-squares in the Midwest; a spread of worn, brick streets through the historic downtown; a wooden post office and city hall that transcend the wear of time; and an equal number of local eateries, chains, churches and bars. The surrounding terrain is mostly deciduous forest and tall-grass prairie, though a rogue band of pine trees frames the northeast along the subsidiary river. A winding stretch of train tracks enters through the bluffs and exits through the west. Faded yellow and orange steam locomotives push coal through Cold Town every ninety minutes, and at the top of the hour during moonlight. The sound is audible from Jonas' house, and he can see them at the Seventh Street crossing, but he considers the trains otherworldly, like ghosts even. He doesn't know where they are going or from where they have come. He doesn't know if conductors sit inside, or if the engines are controlled automatically through satellite and GPS. They travel through the town, never stopping. Here one minute, gone the next.

Cold Town businesses thrive momentarily—a grocer, a coffee shop, an insurance agency—and then they, too, disappear like the trains and storms, and everything else that came in waves of presence and absence. Neighbors would move away for what seemed months before returning as if they had never left. After a fortnight of darkness, the lights of a neighbor's bedroom would shine in the middle of the night for weeks on end, and then suddenly off again, and the cycle would continue.

This town is made of spider web silk, Gwen used to say. Every time you think you've gotten away it draws you back in.

A town will never get me, said Jonas. Forward is my middle name.

———

Seven miles in, and Jonas was running for his life. He had fled into the woods, dodging through elms and ashes at full speed. The man with the rifle had fired at him—once, twice, three times? He couldn't remember. It had happened so quickly. All he knew was that someone was trying to kill him.

A murmur of fire had touched Jonas when he hit the tree-line, a whisper, a moment. It could have been a hornet sting against his shoulder, but there was hot blood coming through a gash in his shirt—real, red, and singing. He couldn't believe it, but there it was.

I've torn myself on a locust tree, he thought. The forest was full of them, their hideous thorns reaching out like barbed teeth.

That's not right, he thought. God help me. I've been shot.

———

One of Jonas' favorite times seemed long ago—the time when Gwen reached the end of her second trimester of pregnancy. He spent hours with his cheek pressed to her firm belly, listening for a sound. He had trouble justifying that something was in there, inside her womb, something alive, and in a few short months, that thing would be living in their house and they would be taking care of it.

Do you think you will like being a mother? he asked her in the middle of the night.

I'm already a mother, she told him without opening her eyes, and she rubbed her hands over her belly for proof. But Jonas couldn't wrap his mind around that idea. Something was inside, sure, but it hadn't taken a breath of fresh air, made a noise, or looked around to orient itself in the world. Something was there, but, then again, something was not.

———

Hiking trails blazed in red surrounded Lake Remote—plastic markers the size of playing cards. Jonas knew the trails well. They crept, twisted, and extended through the forest like the web of glass spreading across a rock-struck windshield. He figured if he could find Lake Remote, even one red mark tacked to a tree, he could get to safety. He could run full speed through the shadows of the forest to the Highway 3 entrance. The monster could never catch him on his home turf. Jonas could find his way back to Eddie and Gwen while the man with the gun felt his way fruitlessly through the trees.

Jonas lost in the timber was a different story. He may as well have been blind. Breathing had failed him. His trained lungs should be full of life, but the air came in and out with little panicked gasps and a needle stabbed him between both sides of his ribs. He could feel his foot bones and skin being punished in the husk of his wet shoes as he crashed against rock and root, his calves as tight as wood; his hamstrings like putty. Blood drained freely from his wounded shoulder, marking his path like a trail of breadcrumbs back to where the man had shot him. Jonas was, for lack of a better term, game. Hunted game.

He couldn't look back, though. There was no time, no time at all. He could only push forward as silently as he could, crunching leaves underfoot and sweeping aside brambles with his good, desperate arm, hoping to stumble across Lake Remote, or something, anything, of familiar shape.

In the distance he heard the faintness of a train whistle. It was coming from the south, moving to his right. He should be able to figure out where he was from the sound and direction, but it only confused him. Where was Cold Town? Where was safety? Why did these woods seem to swallow things, like the day he spent hours hiking the creek bank below the ravine looking for his son's stupid, stuffed dog?

What the fuck is going on, he wanted to scream, all the while wondering if he was, in fact, nowhere near where he thought he should be.

———

A loud crack in the forest. Another gunshot, or was it a tree limb breaking? Was it near or far? Was the man with the gun gaining on him?

Images flooded Jonas' mind. Scenes of love; scenes of violence. Baby Eddie, a bubble on the floor—amorphous and bulging—swaying back and forth, but he cannot, will not crawl. Get Mr. Spots, Jonas tells Eddie. Stop playing around. *Do it*. The calamity of a body torn in half. The pretty girl in tights he had seen during mile two. Part of her on the trail's east side, part of her on the west. Men in dark hats jumping from orange trains with knives in their fists. A spider the size of a muskrat tiptoeing through city streets. Gwen—so anxious, so ready to be elated—clutching his arm in the master bathroom as she waits for the plus sign to appear on the pregnancy test. Baby Eddie army crawling toward his stuffed dog, panting as if he is going 100 miles an hour. Sycamore trees. A clearing. A lake at sunset, the water turned pink. Bullets in the air, spinning clockwise. Gwen, her legs curled around him, hands in his hair, eyes locked onto his. A man with no face pounding on the door in the middle of the night. Eddie, asleep in the baby carrier, his little arms and neck limp.

———

Jonas could run no farther. The forest was too dense, and Lake Remote could not be found. His trail screamed loud and clear—broken sticks, drips of blood. A Boy Scout could have tracked him. He knew that once the man with the gun got him within rifle range, the endgame would begin, and he would be as good as dead, unless he decided to do something drastic.

Jonas took shelter in the first place that presented itself. The cobweb roots of a large cottonwood had outgrown the hill, and they formed a small, natural culvert beneath the trunk—perhaps the size of a badger's den. If the monster did indeed track him to this location, it would be here that Jonas made his stand. The monster would have to take a hand off his gun to navigate the steep grade. When he passed the culvert, Jonas would get him. He'd brain the man with a log. He'd rip the monster's head off.

This is a bogeyman, Jonas thought. The word came to him all of a sudden, like a snapshot slipping out of a photo album and landing on the tiled floor. A bogeyman comes sprinting out of the closet in the middle of the night with long teeth and fingernails. He presses his face against the glass above the kitchen sink while the babysitter crumples against the cabinets and screams until all the screams run out of her lungs. The bogeyman leads little children single-file into the woods, never to be seen again. No one recalls what the bogeyman looks like. They just remember being afraid.

Jonas tried to imagine Eddie being hunted in the hopes that picturing his own son in danger would give him some fatherly courage from deep within—Eddie following the dancing bogeyman to his lair, toddling through the woods with a line of mesmerized children. Eddie's little shape in the crosshairs of a rifle scope. It was horrible to imagine, and it made Jonas sick to his stomach.

What if this was actually the end of his life? What if these were his last few seconds on earth and Eddie grew up without him? Would Eddie remember his dad, the sound of his father's voice, or was he simply too young? Would Eddie only know his dad through photographs and conversation?

Jonas placed a hand to his chest; felt the pounding beneath his ribs. He never remembered it beating so hard. Blood ran from his shoulder. Sweat was everywhere.

Stop crying, he whispered. You fucking child.

He thought of his own dad, an old man now living in Des Moines, Iowa, some 200 miles south—a man who still hunted deer every fall with shotguns and black powder rifles. His dad would know what to do. His dad would be up in a makeshift tree stand, leveling the sights of his twelve-gauge right between the monster's eyes. He'd be in control, armed, calm. Not like Jonas. Jonas never owned a gun. He never punched a man or raised his voice to a stranger. The best Jonas could do was kneel in a puddle of his own piss and tears, clutching a wooden club as if it might be able to save him from a killer with a firearm.

Jonas didn't know what would happen if the monster came around to the low side of the cottonwood. He didn't know if he would see Gwen or Cold Town again. In his mind, all he had was this one chance to prove to his son that he was something that could make its own light, something that could shine on, even in times when dark is darker than dark.

SHELLS

The boy's father tells him there are six different ways a man can kill a duck. A man can park his Ford pickup in a gravel lot, before the sun has risen, and strap a mesh sack of plastic decoys to his shoulders, and walk for miles under the stars, high-stepping through cattails and swamp-grass until he meets a break in the land, a giant puddle of dark shallow water, and he will wait in the weeds for the sun to show, and the little mallards will sleep like floating clumps of grass—eyes closed, breathing watery duck breath onto their tail feathers. A man can spend days on his boat's preparation, stapling vegetation and reeds to wood paneling that he has constructed himself with only a handsaw and hammer, methodically placing each strand under the wire belt until his boat does not look much like a boat at all, but more like a moveable piece of wetland —a strategic island where he and his friends can burst through the slats of the roof and fire steel-shot at swooping teal who circle the decoys, descending slowly like specks of dirt funneling a drain. A man can sneak up on a duck, stepping lightly on wet grass, with one gloved hand on his dog's scruff and the other on his gun's safety, and, without hesitation, unload his firearm at terrified shovelbeaks paddling in a water hole. If he has built a blind on a slough, a man can sleep underneath heavy woolen blankets through the night, wearing thick rubber chest waders, and, with patience, wait for the ducks to come to him. A man can dig a hole and perhaps dress in the color of the earth, white if there is snow, and hide in the sheet-covered hole until flying pintails and big drakes come in from the north to eat leftover corn and grain from the harvested fields. A man can lean out of the Ford F-150's window with a high-powered rifle and pick off floating duck-shapes through a scope without unfastening his seat belt. A man who is truly a man would never do this, the father says.

The father tells the boy that the traditional method of killing a duck is best. "You have to take them by sea, Elliot," the father explains. "I've hunted them that way all my life." It is four-thirty AM. The father motors the boat through the marsh, pushing reeds and cattails aside with the blind-covered bow. The boy, eighteen now and covered head to toe in camouflage, sits in the back of the boat with his eyelids closed, huddled against the sleeping Labrador who smells of urine and wet dog. The father's friend, Dennis, sips black coffee and sits in the boat's middle, straddling a metal box in his 2XL hip-waders.

At the edge of the wetland, they anchor in cover similar to the vegetation nailed on the boat's side panels. Dennis and the father unwind the weights on the bottom of the decoys and toss the plastic ducks overboard. They land in the dark water with a hollow splash. Without the sun on their plastic backs and faces, the decoys look real. They are bird shadows bouncing on tiny waves. "All right, Elliot," the father says. "Best find yourself a hiding spot down there in the weeds. Dennis and I need our shooting room."

The boy does not respond, but climbs out of the boat's stern. His feet sink into mud under ankle-deep water. He worms his way into the tall grass, tromping out a place to sit. From the boat, the Labrador stares back at him, wagging its tail. The pre-dawn horizon is an explosion of pink, blue, and yellow. Opening day, the father has always said, begins with the sun.

The boy remembers a younger time when, before a hunt, he had crawled from his bed a half hour before his father's alarm. He had started the drip coffee, wrapped glazed donuts in tinfoil, and set his knee-boots by the back door, so they could make a quick getaway. He remembers the early nights, lying awake between the covers—anxious to be on the road before daylight—anxious to

94

see the sun rising from the swamp like a ghostly egg yolk. He re-members pressing his mittens against the dashboard heater until the father told him his hands would catch fire. He remembers how different the country roads looked before the sun came up.

––––––

Two weeks earlier the boy decided he would never again kill a duck. He can't do it anymore. He used to shoot at ducks. He used to pep-per their wings and breast-feathers with steel-shot whenever he could. His hands would shake when the father motioned for him to get his head down because a large flock was circling in. If and when he knocked a bird from the sky, the body slapping the water sounded like a football hitting concrete. He turned red-faced with pride the times his father cuffed his shoulder and said, "Damn, El-liot. Fine shell."

In the middle of the night the boy lay awake on the top bunk and pictured the ducks he'd killed, while his roommate, on the bot-tom bunk, made out with a redheaded girl from the fourth floor. Now, the boy decided, he will pull his arm to the left and up when he fires on a duck, and the steel spread will miss the bird, but will scare it enough so it lurches sideways, furiously flapping away from the water—away from the plastic decoys, desperate calls, and ringing shells.

The boy wondered what the father would think if he brought home a vegetarian girl and said that he wanted to marry her. Could the father handle the dinner table when the vegetarian girl referred to the steak in front of her as "charred cow flesh"? The father might toss his cloth napkin aside—always cloth napkins around compa-ny—and he might open the fridge and dig out a brownish celery stalk and a vanilla yogurt carton. Maybe he would set the food in front of the stupefied girl. Maybe he would eat it himself and say, "I guess you could live off it, but I'll stick to my tasty charred cow."

Maybe the boy, himself, would become a vegetarian, grow a beard, stop cutting his hair and start cutting classes. Maybe he would smoke marijuana while sitting Indian-style in a circle with fifteen beautiful girls, and he would let them remove all his clothes and cover his body with herbs and aromatherapy lotion. He could run for state senate under an independent party platform or hitch-hike to South America and work in an orphanage for five years without pay.

The boy traced the cracks in the drywall ceiling above him with a fingertip. In the darkness, the cracks changed into different shapes—tricks of the eye. A rabbit's foot, the profile of a man's face, the curvature of a woman's hips. Underneath him his roommate made love to the redheaded girl from the fourth floor. The pounding on the mattress sounded like footballs bouncing off concrete.

The next morning, the boy woke to a phone call from the father. Over the cell phone the father's voice went on and on. He talked to the boy about the past, what it was like growing up on a farm. He recounted the hard times, the accidents—waking up to a dead sow in the pen—how heavy the carcass was and how, even though it didn't smell or feel like meat, it was enough to feed him and his brothers for weeks. They rolled the body onto a pair of two-by-fours. It took eight hands to lift.

The father's voice explained the unavoidability of dead piglets and lambs. "God always takes a couple," he said. "Usually five percent." When the father was a boy, he had carried the little ones —the stillborn and the dying, the ones that smothered or would not take to teat—out of the barn and laid their bodies in the grass where they could feel the sun on their backs. He could not stand the thought of their disposal, so he sat next to them on the ground, keeping them company, until *his* father, the boy's grandfather, had come over softly in boots and a flannel shirt. The grandfather placed a callused palm on his son's head and said boys can shed tears over livestock; but not men. Men know it won't change facts. Farmers are made to take care of business, the grandfather had said, whether that business was pleasure or pain.

"He was right, you know. It's the way of the world," the father said over the cell phone. "You're in college now, and me and mother are proud of that, but these are things you need to know to become a man."

The boy said he understood, but he cannot connect.

Months from now the father will bring home a button buck during deer season, and the boy will help pull off the hanging buck's skin, but the smell underneath the pelt will overwhelm him and he will sit on the garage's dusty floor with his head between his knees. Even with the garage door open, the sour, dark smell of the meat will be too much, and he will lie down inside the house with his hands over his eyes. He will picture the father butchering the deer alone—the father's cold, red fingers carving the meat. The faraway look in the father's eyes will hurt the boy's insides more than the nausea.

"It would be damn nice if you could be here opening day," the father's voice said through the cell phone. "Me and Dennis got a lead on a spot. Supposed to have drakes big as Canadians."

———

In the cover outside the duck boat, the boy pushes a log underneath his thighs. He positions himself so his buttocks do not sink in the mud. He tries to stay hidden in the weeds while Dennis and the father scan the early morning sky. It is better to be a grebe, he thinks, or a loon, or a cormorant. A grebe can swim silently in the marsh, confused by the shotguns ringing in the distance, but yet, unafraid. Away from the duck boat, the grebe paddles safely in the cove, knowing he is no good for hunting because he is not technically the right fowl. He knows, unlike his distant duck cousin, he is protected by laws, and even though he looks like a duck and swims like a duck, he cannot be shot by a hunter who wants to shoot a duck.

The boy tried to fire at a grebe once, when he was young, but the father yelled him down before the shell left the barrel. The father could not believe his son would dare poach a bird. The boy, not having known better, sat slumped in the boat, blinking back salt. There are rules to hunting, the father had said, rules that can't be broken.

A man should never use lead-shot. Lead bb's sink in the water, and sometimes, for no particular reason, diving ducks and geese swallow them. Their pink tongues push the lead balls down their long necks. They think they are eating food, but really they are poisoning themselves. Three weeks later their feces turn green and their wings droop; they try to skim the surface of the marsh but end up crash landing in the water. Their family flock leaves them behind and they go to sleep in the grass. Sometimes they wake up, but most times not.

A man should never use a rifle for hunting ducks. A rifle should never be fired into the air. They are more sinister than shotguns. They do not release a spread of steel that drops within sight. Rifles shoot bullets—projectiles that travel for miles if not stopped. A bullet that misses the target flies high into the troposphere. Maybe it will puncture the windshield of an aircraft, leaving the pilot limp in his seat, or maybe it will arc like a rainbow and land in a nearby town, perhaps in a playground.

Most importantly, a man should never hunt out-of-season game. The father said that is the biggest sin of all. A man should always respect the animal he's trying to kill.

The sound of Dennis's call booms out from the duck boat. His head is visible just above the blind, and his big neck and throat pulsate as he grunts "Grunk! Grunk! Grunk!" through the duck call. To the west, low on the horizon, a flock of birds circles lazily toward the marsh. The father's call joins in with a chuckle, "Tickatickatickaticka. Grunk! Grunk!"

The boy crouches lower in the weeds. He closes his palm around the cool wood of his duck call. It hangs from a leather cord on his neck. Years ago, the call was given to him as a birthday present by the father. The father had attempted for weeks to teach the boy to call, but the boy could never get the handle of it. "Put it between your lips," the father had said. "Say 'ticket, ticket, ticket.' Faster and faster. And then say 'Ooof, Ooof.' Like you are blowing all the air out of your lungs."

The boy brings the call to his mouth, gathers his breath. Then he lets it fall, and the call swings like a pendulum over his breastbone.

––––––

After the phone conversation with the father, the boy took his food in the dining center, not tasting what he ate. He sat alone next to the window and stared across the courtyard. Outside, the marching band was practicing, blowing wind through brass instruments and banging on drums. He picked at the food on his plate, eating a corncob one kernel at a time, plucking the bread of a ham sandwich from the center. He wondered if the pork between the bread came from a sow that had died on a farm—one that was lifted from the mud on two by fours.

Girls walked by as he chewed his food. There was a career fair going on in the Scheman Building, and many of the girls wore dress suits or skirts. He looked deep into the black fabric surrounding their hips and breasts and wondered what it would be like to lie naked with them on the top bunk. What would they do if he whispered, "I love you" to the back of their heads? Would they notice him? He was not sure.

The father is wrong, he thought. There is more to being a man than maintaining a respect for nature. A man must make his own rules. He must be able to walk up to a girl in a dress suit and tell her she is a brilliant flower—the Swamp Rose Mallow hidden in the verdant tangle of wetland—the sole owner and provider of the tender white petals photographers want to capture, college boys tuck carefully between their sheets, and little woodducks beg to taste. A man must always go after the things he wants.

––––––

A single drake mallard drops low and Dennis and the father snap up their guns, but their steel shots explode behind the buzzing wings. The drake is wounded and lands in the water fifteen yards

99

to the left of the boy. The scent of gunpowder stings the air. The Labrador barks and barks. "Shoot that duck, Elliot," the father says from the boat.

The boy raises his shotgun and sights the mallard down the barrel. He knows if he pulls the trigger, the shell will ignite and he will finish what the father and Dennis have started, but his finger is frozen. In the water, the mallard swims away from the hunters, trying to flap his busted wing. The boy closes his eyes; tugs the trigger. Nothing happens. He checks the safety, squeezes again. Still nothing. "Come on, boy," says the father. "You can't let him suffer like that. Finish him off."

The boy points at the gun, shakes his head. The father motions for him to get down, and the boy crouches. His knuckles turn white as they grip the gun's wooden stock. He cannot see through the weeds, but hears the father shoot twice. The Labrador howls and splashes in the water. "Dead bird," the father says. "Fetch it up."

The boy shakes the gun in his hands. He squeezes it like he wants to crumple it into a ball. Stupid thing, he whispers. Stupid, stupid, thing. He hates the gun. He wants to bury it. He wants to push it down into the soft mud so no one will ever find it again. He points the barrel at the ground and braces his forearms. The cattails in front of him rustle. The weeds part slowly and the wet Labrador's nose sticks through. It wags its thick tail and drops the limp mallard at the boy's feet. The dog looks down at the dead bird, then up at the boy. "Good dog," the boy says. He picks the duck out of the mud and cradles it in his arm like a football. He walks over to the boat and sets it inside the blind.

The father stands up. "Let me see your gun," he says. He takes the over-under from his son's hands and breaks it open. He removes the pair of green cartridges and examines them. "There's your problem," he says. "These here are 20 gauge shells. They won't fire in a 12 gauge. Store must have sold you the wrong ones." He pulls two larger red shells from his coat pocket and eases them into the chambers, slowly, as if he is putting a bottle into a baby's mouth. He closes up the halves of the shotgun. "There you are, Elliot. You're all set now." He offers the loaded gun back to his son.

The boy hesitates. He thinks maybe there will be a better time than this. Maybe that summer when he comes home to visit, the father and he will go fishing at dusk, even though the boy is only in town for several hours. He will tell the father he would rather stay in the house and chat, but the father will assure him that the white bass off Sandpiper Point are biting like hell. The boy will not have a license, but the father will say, "You don't need a license because you're with me."

They might wade in, knee deep, their bare feet muddy and warm between the jagged shore rocks, and they will cast out lines into the gentle waves. Perhaps they do not catch anything, but the wind will rise and a storm will build in the northwest—towering thunderheads rolling past the setting sun. Maybe there will be far-away flashes of lightning, illuminating the river delta that expands into the reservoir's northern shore.

The boy will ask if they should pull in because of the distant lightning. The father will remove his hat and wipe his brow. He'll glance once at the storm clouds. He'll shake his head. He'll say he wants to rest awhile and feel the warm wind on his back. He'll say he wants to keep fishing in the fading light with his son.

Maybe, just maybe, the boy thinks, that is the only thing that matters. He takes the loaded gun from his father's hands and looks to the horizon.

HONEYBEARS

Hurricane James lives on my street, old and rock-bellied and crazy. When the homeboys strut past his stoop he says, "I breathe tougher than you," says it like a copperhead snake staring down the hiss of a big tomcat. He's nothing. The homeboys left a message in his yard—a dead Volkswagen Bug, beat to hell and burned to blackness. They could burn down his house with him inside, and us neighbors wouldn't fill a bucket. None of us would start the hose. Me and Doogan are the only whites that live in this part of town other than Hurricane James. He says this used to be a decent place to live, but the hood sprung up like an "incumbent" garden, homeboys popping out of the cement like rows and rows of cabbage heads. They don't mess with me because I'm real tough to look at. I'm six-feet tall, lean like a billy-club, and scarred in the face. When I was a little kid, I left part of my face hanging on top of a chain-link fence I had just jumped.

One of these days, Hurricane James will get his; he thinks he's tough, sitting on his stoop with his poetry books. Talking shit to little kids with afros. He holds up the books when people walk by as if the dog-eared covers could stop bullets. He knows nothing about tough, nothing about protection. The homeboys are going to gobble him up like a pack of young, shaggy wolves. The newspapers will be all over that—old man, white, dead in the bad part of town. A hate crime. I'll yell out the window to the bees' nest of reporters. I'll say the neighborhood killed Hurricane James. He couldn't hang on, kind of like how leftovers melt off the plate in fancy, suburban dishwashers.

————

Potatoscruff is this cat I have; she's spoiled rotten. Every time I walk in the room, she's hiding somewhere, her beady eyes aglow, watching me like I'm doing something wrong. I'll tell you more about her in a little bit.

I moved to the hood with my friend Doogan, who is the craziest fucker I know. A couple years ago, Doogan was walking along when this giant black dude came down the sidewalk, just minding his own. Doogan got scared and crossed the street to avoid the guy. About halfway to the other side, he had this big revelation. If you hear him tell it, he'll say a big gust of wind blew away the clouds, and the afternoon shined down on his face, and then, like an explosion, a bunch of pigeons came bursting out of the alley like bottle-rockets up the ass. White as doves in the sunlight. So, Doogan stood in the middle of traffic—pigeons, horns, and middle fingers all around him—and felt his heart grow from normal size to six sizes too big. It was like that scene in *How the Grinch Stole Christmas* when old green-fuzzy stared down the mountains at the all the Hoos down in Hooville.

Then Doogan started sprinting and yelling "Sir, Sir!" And the black dude started to run, too, because here was this fat white college kid chasing him. A couple blocks later, Doogan caught up. He shook the guy's hand a whole bunch of times and offered to buy him a cup of coffee or a bagel or lunch. The black dude finally pressed a dollar bill into Doogan's hand. Then he got the hell out of there. Doogan tried to follow, but he was too tired from his earlier sprint. When you are fat like he is, it really slows you down.

Now, Doogan serves as a support-person to the community. Taxpayers pay for his housing, and he hangs out in the worst part of town. When people get robbed or shot or raped, they call him and he figures out what to do. He tries to bring peaceful solutions. He makes people sit in chairs and participate in "constructive dialogues." The guys that hit their girlfriends cry and apologize and say they wish they were dead; they wish that God would turn their fists into pillows. "They are making good progress," Doogan tells me, "really softening up." But a week or two later, the hardness comes back—the tempers, the hitting, the lighting cars on fire in Hurricane James' front yard.

Because Doogan is secretly scared to live alone, Potatoscruff and I stay in the house with him for free, which is fine because people don't mess with me and my scarred face, like I said.

I found Potatoscruff four summers ago on the side of the interstate while driving through Nebraska. She was scrunched up in the shoulder, about to scamper across the highway like Frogger. I pulled over quick, ready to jump in front of traffic rather than see a cat flattened by a minivan. Potatoscruff took one look at me and froze. We were about twenty-five yards apart, staring each other down. I knew exactly what she was thinking. *You'll never take me alive.* I cracked my knuckles; her whiskers quivered. The cars whizzed by. Believe it or not, a tumbleweed rolled between us. Then the chase was on. Potatoscruff was unlucky because there are no trees or hills in Nebraska to hide in, and she was also unlucky because I am a pretty fast guy. After a hundred yards, I plucked her by the scruff and held her high, like a fisher with a trophy bass.

Cats are funny. They don't usually squirm when you get their scruff, and she didn't mind when I carried her to the car and dumped her in the backseat. It wasn't until I started to drive away that she jumped in the back window all shaky and nervous and yowling. Her beady eyes glowed in the rearview. "You'd be dead by now if it weren't for me," I told her.

————

Homeboys have kids sometimes, and Little Elmo is one of them. His father was a mystery, could be one of three or four guys. When you grow into your face, his mom told him, I'll tell you who your daddy is.

I like Little Elmo because he has a giant dome of hair and a big head. He's also too young to take any shit. Doogan says he has spunk. He comes over to my porch sometimes to scratch Pota-toscruff behind the ears. I make peanut butter and honey sandwiches for us. The kid would eat honey every meal if he could. I ask him what he wants to do for a living; he says he wants to be Peyton Manning. That makes me laugh. He asks what's so funny, why would I laugh at a thing like that, and what do I do for a living? I tell him I work for the people whose fence I left part of my face on. They pay me to live here and smoke cigarettes all day. He thinks that's real funny.

Last Christmas, Doogan yelled at me for buying Little Elmo a fifty-dollar Transformers toy. "People need to learn to live with what they have," he said. "Some kid will steal Little Elmo's toy, and all it will do is show him what his mother can't provide." Doogan and I have a serious disconnect when it comes to kids. It's because he's an only child. I won't listen to anyone who is an only child – they think everything they do matters, and everything they say is important. On Christmas Eve, I drank three beers, wrapped the Transformer, and walked over to Little Elmo's house. "To: Little Elmo, From: Peyton Manning" the tag said. I rang the doorbell and left.

Don't ever go near Hurricane James by yourself, I once told Little Elmo. He'll lock you in the closet and feed you broccoli for the rest of your life. Brussels sprouts until you puke.

Little Elmo asked if Hurricane James was the type of guy that would take a kid's hand and put it on his pecker—was he a mean guy like that? No, I said, he's mean. But not like that.

Doogan's problem is that he has to cry every day or he won't feel right. His sobs come out of his bedroom when he thinks I'm asleep. "I'm fine," he says after I knock on the door. "My contacts are old. I think I'm allergic to the cat." Bullshit excuses. There's nothing to say, so I pour him a shot of vodka and he drifts to sleep. Could be any number of reasons he cries every night. I think it has something to do with the fact that he's overweight, lonely, and living in the bad part of town. Or, maybe, he thinks he's actually here to make a difference, and even though he tries and tries, nothing changes. He got a phone call on the night when Billie Redd, a seventeen-year-old kid he knew, died from a bullet to the chest. Doogan didn't cry at all that night. Instead, he sat with me on the porch and talked about baseball, which is funny because I've never seen him watch a game, but he talked like he did. He knew all about the Cardinals, and the Twins, and the White Sox. The guys that played in the field, starting pitchers, hitting coaches, everything. He even explained to me what a balk was, though I still don't understand. When he was a kid he played damn good, he said, he had a real strong arm—a right fielder's arm—and he could hit. Pitchers hated to face him. The worst thing a batter could do to a pitcher is stare him down, not even blink. Pitchers hated that, and Doogan was good at it.

On the worst nights of crying, I pick Potatoscruff off my bed and set her in Doogan's room. Then I close the door.

———

When the homeboys walk by in the daytime, Doogan comes out with a twelve-pack of Coca-Cola and gives each of them a can. I sit on the porch, Potatoscruff in my lap, and let my scars do the talking. Hurricane James looks up from his poetry, pissed off, "I breathe tougher than you." Hurricane James remembers the time when this was a fighting town, and everybody knew who the toughest man in the neighborhood was. He claims he knocked three guys out, the toughest three from surrounding hoods—big German dudes with hair on the knuckles. They took one good punch to the chin, and crumpled like balloons when you let the air out. "Those big Krauts didn't scare me then," he says, "and these young puppies don't scare me now."

He talks and talks, but it's all hot air. A homeboy shot a gun outside his house, one night, when Hurricane James was asleep. The guy was just drunk and firing blankly into the sky, but you could hear Hurricane James inside yelling police, police, oh god, oh. Doogan came hustling out of our house in his t-shirt and underwear, but there was nothing to see. The homeboy had passed out on the sidewalk, the pistol lying beside him. When Doogan tells it, he says the gun looked like a toy—a Matchbox car maybe—that a kid had fallen asleep on the floor playing with. Doogan put the gun in the dumpster and rolled the guy onto his side, then he made a phone call. I tried to listen, but he talked too quiet.

———

Little Elmo is really into honeybears. He has a collection of them. Whenever anyone finishes a bottle of honey, Little Elmo will be at their door in less than a day asking for the empty bear. I don't know how he knows these things; the kid's got a sixth sense. He fills the bears with different materials—cotton balls inside makes a polar bear—and names them Buzz or Buster or Banana-eater, always with a B. If I feed him a peanut-butter-and-honey sandwich, he makes me show him the bottle to see how much honey is left. "A couple more days," he'll say, "that bear will be empty, and then I'll have to have him."

I always ask what kind of bear it will be. "That one's a big grizzly," he'll say. "A real man-eater" or "That's just another black one, but he turns invisible when he wants to."

One time he went to collect a honeybear from Hurricane James. The old man asked Little Elmo if he was going to make a bong out of it, then he busted up laughing. Doogan and I were sitting on the porch doing the crossword. I had one eye out, making sure no funny business happened. Doogan looked up when Hurricane James started to laugh. He said to me in a quiet voice that people shouldn't say things like that to kids because they are very impressionable.

———

This used to be a nice part of town about thirty-five years ago. The houses were made of brick, and thick grass grew in the lawns. Some of these twisted trees used to have great big leaves, nine months a year. Now, I guess they are just skeletons of what used to be. The worst part is the color of everything. I can't put my finger on what to call it. It's like when you have a nice white t-shirt that gets dirty. No matter how many times you wash it, it will never be white again. That's how things look around here: the cars, the bricks, the cement—washed out. Even Potatoscruff, who used to have such a fine, striped coat, is getting pretty drab because she doesn't clean herself.

Sometimes I bring home fresh-cut flowers, gerber daisies and pink carnations, just to add a little color. This one time Doogan saw the vase full of flowers and asked if I bought them for a lady, and did she have any friends that would find him interesting. I told him to grow some nuts and hit the gym. He didn't think that was funny. It's because kids used to ask him what bra size he wore. That's a shame, I said, kids can be total bastards. "It's not their fault," he said, "kids can be very impressionable."

Doogan cried himself to sleep that night. Potatoscruff snuck out of my room and ate the petals off all the flowers.

———

The homeboys took offense to Hurricane James, one afternoon, when he called the police on them. He stood on his stoop with his cell-phone, a smug grin on his old face, and dialed the cops right in front of their noses. The homeboys were out in the sun, having a smoke and listening to music at a house across the street. They sipped from the cans of Coke that Doogan ran out to them, unaware that the police were speeding their way because Hurricane James squealed that a small gang of colored boys was outside smoking dope and throwing bricks at cars and houses and people.

There wasn't much Doogan could do when the cops showed. He stood between the police and the homeboys with his arms raised as if he were trying to stop the walls of a treehouse from collapsing. Eventually, someone spit in the face of a cop, and then out came the billy-club, and a homeboy was on the ground holding the sides of his head and rolling from stomach to back, back to stomach. The cops took him away. Doogan talked the rest of the homeboys into getting the hell out of there. But they didn't leave for long.

They came back at night when the street was asleep. Everybody knew they were coming. They stole a Volkswagen Bug, and parked it in Hurricane James' front yard. They went to work on the car, beating it first with bats and crowbars and rocks, and then hosing it down with gas. One of them dropped a lit match into the wreck. My windowpane filled with light. Potatoscruff looked out the glass, her eyes orange from the glow. She watched as the car burned and the homeboys danced in the flames and yelled at the front of Hurricane James' house. They dared him to call the police again. "Just call," they yelled, "we want you to call. We promise you won't regret it."

I'm sure Hurricane James lay down in his bathtub that night with his clothes on. I'm sure he held his poetry books to his chest and concentrated on breathing—not all the noise outside—just the simple act of letting the air in and out of his lungs. I shooed Potatoscruff away from the window and closed the blinds. Even Doogan didn't go outside that night. I can't say I blame him.

———

Billie Redd, the seventeen-year-old who died from a bullet to the chest, was Doogan's only friend besides me. Doogan and Billie Redd would eat potato chips and watch *The Simpsons* together every night in our living room. Billie Redd never much wanted to be a homeboy, but all the homeboys liked him enough, so they talked him into it. To make Billie Redd a man, the homeboys dropped five dollars in change on the pavement, and then they beat him until he picked all the coins up. He came over to our house that night, and I gave him beers until his back and chest and arms stopped hurting. He drank the beers slowly, cradling a bag of frozen peas against his forehead and scratching on Potatoscruff's back with his free hand. He said he was glad that I was scarred in the face, but he felt sorry that I knew what it was like to get stared at.

109

When Doogan got home, he took one look at me and Billie Redd drinking beers; then he went right into his bedroom and locked the door. We sat for over an hour, sipping drinks, until Doogan came out. He had a big envelope full of something. His face was all white, like the way people look who haven't eaten anything in a couple of days. "You promised me, man," he kept saying. "I believed you."

He touched Billie Redd's swollen forehead. "Does that hurt?"

Billie Redd shrugged. "You don't know how it is," he said. He had such a quiet voice. Quiet and calm like an old man. "Sometimes there aren't a lot of choices."

"No," said Doogan. "There's always a choice. You just have to see it."

He set the envelope on the table. Billie Redd thumbed through the contents. "I can't take this," he said. "You can't buy someone out of trouble."

"Give it to them," Doogan said, "and say you're out. Tell them you're finished."

Billie Redd shook his head. "That's not going to work. They'll pull me back in."

"Then *you* take it," Doogan said, "and tell me you'll run away forever."

———

One of my worst dreams happened on the night when the homeboys beat and lit the car on fire in Hurricane James' front yard. The strange part is that I dreamed the most beautiful colors you ever saw—golds and greens and yellows. In the dream, the homeboys gathered outside Hurricane James' house, but instead of bringing in a car, they kicked down the door and pulled him out. They tied him to the trunk of the neighborhood's biggest oak tree. But unlike reality, this oak had leaves the size of pillowcases, the most brilliant color of green. I knew what was going to happen as soon as they tied him up, one of those dreams where you tried not to watch, but you couldn't look away. The part that disturbed me most was when Billie Redd stepped forward. I expected his soft, calm voice to make things right, order Hurricane James untied. But when he opened his mouth, tendrils of fire came shooting out like crimson snakes. They engulfed everything they touched—Hurricane James, the tree, the houses behind.

Then the dream made me look away. It stuck my eyes to the top of that burning tree. I wanted it to stop; wanted to call Doogan or the police or the fire department, anyone who would make the flames go away. But it was the type of dream where you couldn't move and you couldn't yell. As I watched, those leaves melted one by one into curled, gray shells, the kind that twist in the wind and break off piece by piece until there's nothing left.

The next morning, Hurricane James told me that every time homeboys kill one of their own, it warrants a little prayer of thanks. It's like people on death row committing suicide, he said. I wasn't talking to him, I was carrying in groceries, and I heard that cold, reptile voice of his. When I turned around, he was sitting on his stoop, an open poetry book on his knee, looking directly at my face. In his yard, the dead car had turned completely black—a corpse of metal, melted rubber, and ash. A shiver went up my spine.

Him staring at me like that made the scars on my cheeks burn, a real deep kind of feeling that started inches behind my face. I hurried toward the house. He said, "This neighborhood would fall to pieces if there weren't folks like me who stand up to the bad people."

He laughed and closed his poetry book. "Stop fooling yourself. You guys would be dead by now, if it wasn't for me."

———

Little Elmo showed up at the house with one of his honeybears the day after Billie Redd was shot to death. I was on the porch listening to Doogan talk about when a centerfielder should throw to second base and when he should throw home, when I saw Little Elmo's big dome of hair bobbing above the porch spindles.

"What's happening, my man?" Doogan said.

"Oh, nothing much."

"Does your mom know you're over here?"

"No." Little Elmo sat down cross-legged. "Does your mom know you're here?"

Doogan shrugged. Little Elmo ignored us and played with his honeybear, this one filled with sand. He bounced it all over the porch, making it jump over lasers and do battle with an army's worth of bad guys that only he could see. Doogan started his baseball talk again, but stopped to watch. I watched, too. Even Potatoscruff, who had been asleep on my lap, perked her ears and had a look. Little Elmo stood up. "Oh, no," he said. Holding the honeybear up like a shield, he backed himself into the corner, as if he were being overwhelmed by a porch full of enemies. "Okay, Buzz," he said to the bear, "looks like there's too many of them. It's time to go invisible."

He made a noise like a dishwasher makes when you open the door and it's still running. Then he slipped the honeybear beneath his shirt. I looked over at Doogan. He had his hands in his face like he was getting ready to cry, but nothing was coming out. No tears. Doogan just sat there, silently, pressing his palms into his eyeballs. His lips moved as if saying something he didn't want anyone to hear, but other than that, he didn't make a sound. I reached out my hand to touch his shoulder, but stopped halfway.

Doogan didn't understand. Not really. He didn't have scars. Didn't have bears or poetry. To him, the neighborhood still had color. Soon enough he'd be like me, an observer, enjoying the pleasure of a cool breeze, a fuzzy cat on the lap. In a year or so, he'll stop seeing them, stop crying. Billie Redd will be just a memory. Hurricane James will follow. And each week Little Elmo will fade more and more, until one day, he and his honeybears actually do disappear. That will happen later, when Doogan is over all this. But right now, he needed to feel it.

"What's this guy's problem?" Little Elmo asked.

BUGS

Mom says bugs are Satan's minions. I believe her because she has red hair with streaks of gray in it. She's older than me by seventeen years. "The big four-five, Joe," she tells me. "That's how old I've gotten." I love Mom because she hands me a paper towel and says, don't kill him. Put him in the woods where he belongs. I pick up the crickets, and the roaches, and those little Chinese beetles that pretend to be ladybugs. I open the sliding glass door and flick them towards freedom. When I come back inside she says thank you, sweetheart. I like to hear that. When I turn forty-five, I want gray streaks in my hair, too. Right now, I am the big two-eight, and my hair is just brown.

Mom won't let me cook hamburgers in the house. She smells the meat getting up in her pretty, red hair. They don't make a shampoo to remove that smell, but I could earn a good living if I invented it, she thinks. I wouldn't even know where to start. What do I know about shampoo? On Friday nights Mom washes her hair, and we go to the movie theatre and take in a double feature. I eat popcorn and Junior Mints until my guts hurt. I ask her to rub my back. She reaches behind, and I feel her strong fingers working all the kinks and knots out, making the hurts disappear. It feels like a sunny day.

Old Man stopped coming around so much after Mom had her fall on the stairs. Aunt Cat swears Old Man pushed Mom. I don't know what to believe. Aunt Cat was terrible mad in the hospital.

Unquestionably furious, she called it. She yelled bad words so loud that her voice chased Old Man out of the hospital room—chased him down the hall, into the elevator, and across the parking lot. Bad words that turned my ears red, made the nurses pop their heads out from behind those curtains. Old Man kept saying, "Now look here, look here," but that didn't stop Aunt Cat. She even yelled bad words while he drove away, both hands on her hips; her hair did somersaults and cartwheels in the wind. I think she believed those words would catch him.

I heard Mom say a bad word only once in my life. This was in the hospital parking lot when I pushed her chair out to the van. The doctors said she was ready to go home. I picked her up in my arms and asked, did Old Man actually push her down the stairs or did she slip? As I set her in the front seat, she touched my face. "Joe," she said in a soft way. "I don't want you to ask me that. Because, in the end, it don't fucking matter. Not one bit." My face got warm because I thought she was sore at me for asking, but she made sure I understood she wasn't. We stopped at McDonalds on the way home. She said to order three double cheeseburgers for me, some fries, and a big chocolate shake for her. The strange part is she didn't take a sip of her shake. She just held it in her hands and looked out the window.

What I like about Mom, now, is she lets me drive everywhere we go. She likes to ride in the van, especially in the summer time. It feels good to move, she says. We listen to Neil Young and put the windows down. I drive us through the countryside, a scenic place is what she wants. She doesn't like lakes so much, but she's a fan of rivers. She likes wind, too. That's her favorite. A strong wind blowing against a willow tree is just about the best thing in the world to look at, she thinks. I'm not impressed by a bunch of stringy leaves swinging and whipping in the breeze. Maybe we ought to drive to Florida, I tell her. I'll build us a house made of bricks and you can sit in the chair and watch hurricanes. She'd see so much wind, she'd be sick of it. That would sure be something to own a house in Florida, Mom thinks.

Old Man owns a diner on Eighth Street. Before Mom fell down

the stairs, he worked the dinner shift every night. He always wore a flannel shirt, white apron, and a Boston Red Sox hat turned backwards. Mom and I'd go there on weeknights and he'd give us a basket of fries and chicken strips. He'd lean his elbows on the counter, his chin in his hands, and say, "Can I get you anything else, Congressman? How about for your younger sister?" I laughed and laughed at that. Who would think Mom looked younger than me? What kind of guy would call me Congressman?

She and Old Man were going steady back then. After his shift, Old Man would come over to watch *David Letterman*. At the end of the top ten list, I'd head for the sack and he'd still be there. "Night, Joe," he'd say. "I'll be leaving in a little bit after I tuck your mother in." I'd go to my bedroom and press my ear against the door. I could hear Mom laughing, and Old Man calling her his sweet little girl. He smelled like hamburgers after he worked the dinner shift. I liked that about him.

I liked it when he called me Congressman, too. Imagine me working for the President. I could fill the machines in the White House. I bet that'd be a great job. Those fancy bottles of water. Health snacks. Machines where you pay with plastic cards. When the president walked by, I'd say "Coca-Cola, sir?" and hold out an ice-cold can for him. He'd say, "Keep up the good work, Joe." Filling the machines at the university is nice, except when the students walk by and snag a Mountain Dew or a bag of chips when I'm loading up. My boss wants to know why he shouldn't think I took the things that were stolen. I hold up my hands and try to explain it again. He laughs and says that I can always have a soda or chips. I don't even have to ask. "Just take one, Joe," he says. "You work hard for that money. Have one. Go ahead." My boss is a strange guy. He knows I'd never steal.

Money is what Old Man tried to give me when Mom fell down the stairs. I was in my room listening to Patsy Cline on the CD player. I heard Old Man yelling at Mom in the kitchen. He had been out to the bar that night, and he was saying that she ought to let him have another drink, but Mom absolutely would not. That's her strongest rule. She never lets me touch a drop, either, which is fine because beer tastes like Dr. Pepper that sat in the sun too long. Whiskey is even worse.

When I heard Mom tumble down the stairs it sounded like a big tree falling over, or a baseball breaking through an expensive window. I ran to the kitchen. Down in the basement, Mom lay on her back. Her eyes were closed and her hands were shaking. Her gray and red hair was all fanned out. She didn't scream or nothing. Just waved her arms and breathed hard, like she couldn't get enough air. I yelled down to see if she was okay, but it hurt too much to answer.

Old Man was crying at me. He had his hands on my shoulders, and he said "Joe, you got to understand, I just took one step forward and she took one step back. I wouldn't hurt your Mom, not on my life. Believe me, Joe." I was too busy hustling down the stairs and picking Mom up in my arms to listen. I carried her next door to Aunt Cat's.

Mom kept falling asleep and waking up on Aunt Cat's couch as we waited for the ambulance truck. She'd look at me and say, "My foot fell asleep, Joe. Can you come rub it?" I sat next to her and massaged her feet while she drifted in and out. Her feet felt cold and dry. They didn't move a bit, even when I ran my fingers over the bottom, even when I pressed hard to make them wake up.

Old Man came inside before the ambulance showed. He had a whole bunch of cash, wrapped in a rubber band. He took me into Aunt Cat's bedroom and said. "Joe, I think you ought to take this money." I asked, why would he want to give me all that cash? He said, "It ain't wrong to take it. I just feel awful, and I wish you would have it. You can take it, can't you? Take it and tell me you think I'm not a bad guy."

His eyes were swelled up, red, like he'd been rubbing them all night. "Say you wouldn't be ashamed if I was your Dad. Say you'd be proud if I called you my son. Can you say that for me, Congressman?"

I thought for sure he'd start crying again, so I folded the money and put it in his shirt pocket. I told him he wasn't my dad, but I thought he was a pretty swell guy. I said he should give the money to Mom so she could buy a pretty dress or a nice bird feeder. She could buy some of those expensive shoes she's always looking at.

Old Man left after I said that. I didn't see him again until Aunt Cat screamed all those bad words in the hospital.

Mom says I am her best soldier. I like to hear that. She says, unlike the other guys in her life, I will go to war for her. I'm the one who saves her from the scary bugs that come into our house. Imagine me in an army captain's helmet, picking up the roaches, and crickets, and box elder bugs with paper towels, protecting Mom from them crawling on her. I used to kill the bugs when Mom wasn't looking, because it's easier than putting them outside. But, I changed my ways because I know it upsets her. It's terrible to see Mom upset. She goes into hibernation like a bear. Lays around, won't eat, won't talk. Like a dead thing on the couch. Wake up, Miss Grizzly, I tell her. I open the curtains. I turn on the TV, put in her favorite tapes, but it won't help. She says you just have to let things take their course, let the bad feelings drain out of your body.

The worst time was the two weeks after we got back from the hospital. Mom wouldn't talk at all. My boss gave me leave to be with her, which is funny because I didn't fill in a request. He just told me I was on vacation. Mom didn't say more than five words. She slept on the couch almost the whole time, wouldn't get in her chair. She was so weak I had to carry her to the bathroom. When she reached out her arm and touched my knee, I knew she had to go. Aunt Cat brought over food, and we'd all eat together. The tv was on the whole time, but Mom didn't care what we watched. I left the channel on ESPN for two hours, once, and we watched the same episode of *SportsCenter* back to back. Mom hates sports.

Here are two things about Old Man that I probably shouldn't say. The first thing is that he still comes over to our house late at night when I'm supposed to be asleep. I can hear him and Mom talking in her bedroom. They sleep on the bed together. I can hear the bed move when he lies down, and when he rolls over. Sometimes he moves around a lot. I know what's going on. When I get up the next day, Mom's already in her chair. The bed's made. Old Man is long gone.

The second thing I probably shouldn't say is that sometimes I feel like killing him. I don't know why I feel that way, never felt it towards anyone before, but Old Man brings it out in me. It's like, if I found him in the morning going out to his pickup truck, I'd tackle him, and I'd sink my fists into his face, and pull his hair, and gouge his eyeballs out. I'd keep hitting him until he died, until the lawn was covered in his blood. I'd probably have to bury him in the back garden and sneak in through the basement door, so Mom didn't see. I'd wash off in the slop sink and come up with a good story before going upstairs. When Mom asked if I'd seen Old Man around lately, I might say "It don't fucking matter" like she said in the hospital parking lot. But, of course, I don't have the guts. I don't have it in me to kill Old Man. I can't even kill those stupid bugs that sneak into Mom's room anymore. Besides, sometimes I think he's a pretty swell guy. He gives me a hamburger on the house if I swing by the diner. He looks me in the eye, shakes my hand, and calls me Congressman.

Mom told me, when I asked if Old Man still came around, that she was going to die one day. I don't know why she said it. We were sitting outside drinking good lemonade, and Mom was watching the wind move through the leaves. She said, "When I die, Joe, who is going to take care of you? Who is going to love you like I do?" She was in one of her down moods, where nothing could cheer her up. Her eyes had a faraway look, like they were caught in the breeze, flying miles and miles past the backyard. I told Mom that Aunt Cat would take care of me. She would love me. But Mom said that wouldn't be enough. "You could find someone, Joe," she said. "We could find someone to love you. You'd like that, wouldn't you? A nice girlfriend? A girl you could call sweetheart?" I thought that was funny. Imagine me with a girlfriend, buying flowers, and taking her out for steak dinners. I told her that would never work. I wouldn't know what to say, wouldn't know how to act. Besides, I liked the way things were, now.

118

It got me thinking, though. What would it be like to go steady with a girl? Mom says that when you are in love, your mind goes bye, bye. You do things you don't normally do. Talk mushy, and hug, and kiss, and say things like "I missed you when you went into the other room." She says sometimes love makes you hurt the people you care about. I suppose I wouldn't mind being in love so much, as long as the girl liked the same tv shows I liked, the same type of music. If Mom thought she was a good girl, I could probably marry her. To be honest, I'd rather just hang out with Mom than spend time with somebody that didn't know me. Plus, a girl wouldn't like to sleep in the same bed as me because I toss and snore all night long, and I turn on the lamp when I have bad dreams. If I had a wife, it would be nice to sleep naked together at night, I think, with all the lights off and the windows open. The guys at work say it feels best in the dark because your eyes can't see to mess things up.

Sometimes, Mom and I go for drives at night. These drives are my favorite. There's not much to see except what's in front of the headlights. Maybe look at the stars. We buy fries or chips and a couple Cokes, and we drive around for hours, just listening to the radio and feeling the cracks in the road go bump, bump under our seats. Mom takes my hand when she finishes her fries. She turns up the radio on her favorite songs. "My Joe," she says.

I went to see Old Man last week, all by myself. Mom doesn't know about this. "Congressman, how you doing?" he said when I walked in the diner. I had my tough face on, and I ordered a beer and a hamburger, cooked well done. "Joe," he said. "You know we ain't got beer here. Besides, your mom would lock you out for days if she knew you were drinking." I told him I didn't care if it was on the menu. I wanted a beer.

He went into the back and come out with a bottle of Miller Lite. He twisted the cap off and set it in front of me. "It's warm," he said. I told him that was how I liked it, and took a big drink. It tasted awful, but I didn't make a face. "Bad day?" he asked.

I told him, yeah. Some kids had walked by while I was filling up the machines and swiped a case of Mountain Dew. When I yelled

119

after them, they turned and said, "Stupid retard." I told him I had gotten terrible angry, like I was ready to do some real damage. I rolled my sleeves so Old Man could see my big arms, all the veins popping out. Then, I don't know why I made this up, but I said I chased after those kids, caught up to them in their dorm. I said, I told those kids to give me the Mountain Dew or I'd knock them out, beat them until they turned black and blue.

But none of that really happened. What happened was I ran the cart back to the boss, and he gave me the rest of the afternoon off. He said college boys don't have any balls or manners. I kept thinking about how much I hated those words, "stupid retard." I wish those kids had said it when the boss was around. He might have kicked them out of college. He might have let me pour a two-liter of Mountain Dew in their backpacks. The more I thought about it, the more I felt like going to see Old Man. I don't know why. It wasn't his fault those boys said that.

"So, did they give it back?" Old Man asked.

I told him, of course they did. It's because they were afraid of me. It's because I'm a pretty strong guy. The type of guy you don't want to mess with. I took another big drink of beer and looked Old Man right in the eyes. He nodded and said, "You sure showed them, Joe."

After I finished eating, Old Man said like he always does that the burger was on the house. But I dropped a twenty dollar bill on my empty plate and walked out without saying goodbye.

Mom likes it when I run in the yard. We'll be sitting out back, and she'll smile in a playful way. If I see that smile, I know what's next. She says, "Go ahead, Joe, run for me." I try to cop out. I say that my back hurts or my legs feel sore, but she won't have none of it. She starts sweet talking me, saying "Oh, please, don't you want to run for your poor old mother? Don't you want to stretch them legs?"

I stand in the grass with my shoes off. I kneel down in a crouch like a track star, and when Mom says "Ready, set, go" I take off and run a lap around the yard. I feel kind of funny when I do it, but she gets such a thrill from watching that I don't mind.

Every time, I try to go faster and faster, until my feet are numb from hitting the ground, and the wind stings my eyes so I can't see nothing but a blur of clouds and sun, and all I can hear as I turn the corner and chug for the next is Mom's voice yelling "Faster, Joe! Faster! You can do it. I know you can!"

When I finish the run, I stand next to her with my hands on my knees. My breath is heavy, and the sweat drips off my face. Her strong fingers move to my back and start to work the knots out. Her fingers travel up and down my spine. They find the hurts and make them disappear.

GHOSTWATER

Heroin is never a good thing, Uncle Bones says. His hands are on my mom's hands. They move to her shoulders. Now they're wrapped around her stomach, and he's resting his chin on her head. I am sitting in the recliner watching *The Surreal Life* on VH1, a bottle of Cherry Coke in my hand, a plate of Swiss cheese and crackers on my lap. Uncle Bones' long dark hair flanks my mom's face. It looks like she's wearing a wig.

"Uncle Bones, what do you know about heroin?" I say.

He tells me he knows plenty.

I have hated Uncle Bones for four days, from the moment I came home. When I walked into the living room with my suitcase, he had his legs spread on the couch cushions. His black jeans and gray underwear lay crumpled on the carpet. His head was tilted back and his lips were open, like ready to catch a tennis ball in the mouth. My mom knelt between his knees. Both of her hands moved up and down on his purple little member. My suitcase hit the floor. They covered each other up. They said things like "Jesus, boy. Close the door" and "Jack, Sweetheart, what are you doing home?"

"I used to do a thing or two," says Uncle Bones, "back in the 80's. Shit your dad wouldn't touch."

On tv, Flavor Flav chases Brigitte Nielsen. He feels her ass with skinny, dark hands. I eat a cracker.

"Bet you did a little H," says Uncle Bones, "when you hung out with your brother. Bet you guys took the ride together a time or two."

"Stephen," says my mom. Stephen is Uncle Bones' real name. She touches his face, his thin mustache. Her lips puff, but he doesn't kiss her. He looks at me instead.

That's when I lose it. I give him what he wants: a real lunatic show. There's loud noise everywhere, some of it from my mouth. I spit on the carpet. Crackers and Swiss cheese fly across the room. The crackers burst against the wall. The cheese sticks for a moment, then trickles down like square white tears. A puddle of Cherry Coke soaks into the rug, and Uncle Bones stands between me and my mom. She cries and cries. He tells me to step down, step down before he puts me down. I tell him the only one in this house he's allowed to fuck is himself. His cheeks turn red, and then they turn white. His fists are in my face but I can't feel them.

———

My brother took his own life. His ghost is in the ceiling. Watching me. I write these words on a blank sheet of printer paper. I am alone in my room. I cross out the first sentence, and instead write, *My brother murdered himself.*

I look up. *Nathanial in the attic. Blue lips and bruises. Bloody eyes. Pulls the tourniquet tight, sticks the needle in. Here comes the heroin, boy. Bet you didn't know it was going to kill you. Bet you didn't know you'd be stuck above my room, you ghost.*

I stand on my bed and pin the sheet of paper on the ceiling next to the others. This is what I do now. The ceiling is covered with pictures I have drawn. Words about my brother. Lists, stories, memories, sketches. Black ink on white. Some papers are separated. Others overlap. The ceiling looks like the floor of a mad novelist's study. It looks like a ream of paper gave up on life, took a swan dive off the rooftop.

———

123

Most people begin their process of addiction with cigarettes and alcohol. Not my older brother Nathanial. He chose to huff rubber cement and gasoline from a pair of pink panties he kept in his sock drawer, a souvenir from his first girlfriend. He soaked the panties in gas from the jug in the garage, spooned rubber cement in the middle, and wadded the mess into a ball. Then he spread the panties over his face.

I was fourteen at the time, sitting on the floor and watching. He was seventeen. I could tell it was working because he said his hands were turning into flippers.

"Like a fish?" I asked.

Not a fish, he said. It was more like a turtle. Big green turtle flippers.

"Really?"

He pulled the panties from his face, shrugged. He said that everything moved in slow motion for a couple seconds, and he heard a weird ringing sound. That was about it. The part about the flippers, he had made up.

I asked if I could try, but he said no. This wasn't something I should get involved in. Older brothers are supposed to protect the younger ones. When I was man enough, then I could try. We could do it together. In a year or two, I'd be plenty old by then.

But Nathaniel was lying. Big brothers always lie. He didn't let me try anything, not even a hit of marijuana, no matter how old I got. In the woods at the edge of town, I watched him vomit from eating puffball mushrooms the size of softballs. He sprayed aerosols up his nose. Tried cocaine. After fasting twenty-four hours, he drank a bottle of Nyquil. The next day, he dropped 500 micrograms of acid and saw spiders climbing the wall in single file. Every time I asked for a taste, he said I wouldn't enjoy it. Slapped the side of my head and told me to get real. Good boys like me shouldn't get into that type of shit. Bad boys like him, when they turned nineteen, stripped down to their underwear and walked into a downtown warehouse. The type of warehouse where a white kid could buy low-grade heroin, if he could prove he wasn't a tattletale.

Three years ago, Nathanial injected spiked heroin. His heart stopped less than a minute later. The doctors called it a massive myocardial infarction. He was twenty years and five days old. After his funeral, I left town for good. Seemed like the right thing to do. But I came back on my twentieth birthday. That was four days ago. I wanted to be home when I outlived him.

Tomorrow, I will be exactly as old as Nathanial when he died.

————

At three AM, I drive my car to the river, my jean pockets stuffed full of change. Led Zeppelin plays softly over the stereo. The river runs through the west side of town, its water thick, dark, and alive between the banks. In March, the land north of here floods, and the stream swells up the concrete levee wall. I open the car door. Ever since moving home, I've come here at three AM to stand above the water on the pavement.

I pull quarters, nickels, and dimes from my pockets and hold them over the current. The coins tumble from my palms and turn end over end. Their shadows flit along the levee walls before they land like silver raindrops, and are swept away in cold water. I imagine the coins, the faces of men dead for decades, sinking and spinning as the river carries them away, to another town perhaps, or a muddy grave.

I think about Nathanial. I picture his face on the coins, trapped in a circle less than an inch wide. I think about him sinking in the water.

————

Uncle Bones visits my room the next afternoon. He stares at the drawings and writings pinned to the ceiling. The block letters on his coffee mug say, "I used to care, but now I take a pill for that."

"Eye looks better," he tells me. "You really went off the deep end last night."

I tuck my pen behind my ear. I ask if he has anything better to do with his weekdays.

"Me and your mom are heading down to Altoona tonight. Gonna win some of that tax money back at Prairie Meadows."

He looks at one of the pages on the ceiling, shakes his head, then stares out the window. The March clouds hang dark and low. "It's been like this for days," he says. "Looks like a storm building, but nothing of it. I wish it would rain. Sure could use one—help clean the crazy out of this place.

"Your dad used to tell me," he continues, "if it rains hard enough, it can wash away the graves. That's when dead people climb out their coffins. Got no skin. Worms coming out of every such place. They walk the streets, looking for their families. Like they don't know they're dead. Used to scare the shit out of me every time it rained. Rain hit the roof and your dad would whisper, 'That's footsteps, ain't it?' I spent half my childhood terrified of weather."

I say, "And now you're sleeping with his ex-wife to get back at him? Is that why you're here, Uncle Bones?"

He sets down his mug. "Me and your mother are in love," he says. His long hair jangles when he says the word *love*. "Don't make an ocean out of a puddle."

He picks up the cup and slurps. "It was a load of piss anyway, what your dad told me. Rained so hard once it unearthed half the caskets in the cemetery cross town. Nobody climbed out the boxes. Dead people stay dead."

He points to the papers on the ceiling. "You're scaring your mother. Putting poems and shit on the walls. Nathanial was my nephew, too. He was my blood, just like you are. He was the one: put that needle in his arm, chose to inject poison. And he paid the price. No sense in denial; it's plain facts."

I tell him he's right so he'll shut up. He nods, stares out the window, and sips his coffee. Uncle Bones is an infection festering on an open sore. He is the bits of foil-wrap stuck to a chocolate bar. He is the black sheep that shits and bleats everywhere it goes.

"It ain't gonna rain," he says.

————

As my mom and Uncle Bones drive the Chevy toward Prairie Meadows, my brother's ghost begins to cry in the attic above my bedroom. At first it is soft, like wind brushing through leaves, then louder. I press my face into the pillow and wait for him to stop, but he doesn't.

When I roll over, the room is dark. I can hear "pock. pock." on the papers above, as if the drawings and writings are catching his tears. Little paper umbrellas.

He is directly above me now, scratching at the other side of the ceiling. Trying to get to me. He wants me to join his sadness, but I won't. Poor dead brother. Killed himself with nobody watching. No one around to worship him. No one to ask what dying feels like.

"Shut up, Nathanial," I say. "Shut the fuck up."

I hold my breath and listen. All he does is cry.

Part of me isn't sorry he's gone. There's a reason why I stayed in the parking lot during his funeral, a reason why, when my mom took my arm and urged me inside, I sat on the pavement. I wasn't moving. Anybody tried to help me up, I turned my body into lead.

————

The first night he tried heroin, Nathanial made me tie him to a rocking chair. We were up in the attic. Three AM on my sixteenth birthday.

I didn't like the idea at all. Didn't like needles. Didn't like the word *heroin*. It was a word the fat-necked cop who came to school every year used to illustrate just how bad drugs can be. He showed us videos of people strung out on smack, Angel Dust. Addicts strapped to a stretcher, their knuckles bloody from punching walls or windows or family members. They couldn't stop shaking, yelling, trying to break their restraints. The cop nodded as the video played. "See that?" he said. He hit rewind. "See?"

Nathanial fixed the tourniquet against his bicep. His veins pushed out like thin worms stretching toward his wrist. I didn't watch the needle go in.

He gritted his teeth and said Jesus Christ, Jack. Jesus Christ. He couldn't do this with me looking at him like that. He needed to be alone. I tried to argue, but he didn't hear me. I climbed the ladder down to my room.

He sat on my bed when it was over. His eyes looked like drips of blood.

He couldn't stop talking nonsense. He said that heroin was like a flood breaking inside you. When you punctured the skin, it was an opening for everything to come in. It filled you up like a reservoir—the outside, the heroin. Made you invincible. That was my birthday present. Invincible Nathanial could take away my pain. He promised me that. All I had to do was think about him, and the pain would leave my body and go into his. He could always protect little Jack, he said. Always, always.

———

In my dreams that night I am riding a motorcycle toward my house. The sky is horror-movie black, and the wind is howling. Uncle Bones is standing on the front porch, but he doesn't have any arms. His long hair blows sideways. He's wearing a sleeveless shirt, and his smooth arm-stumps wiggle as he waves me inside.

When I walk into the living room, all the furniture is overturned. My mom is hiding behind the couch, screaming. She can hear Nathanial walking down the stairs. Don't let him come down, she says. Her hands cover her eyes.

I can hear it, too. His breathing. His feet taking the steps one at a time. I turn, ready to face him, but there's nobody in the stairwell. No dead brother. Nothing to see but shitty carpet.

———

Morning comes. I find myself at the kitchen table sitting across from my mom. She is baking muffins and talking about racehorses. She says, "It's almost unreal how strong they are. Like nothing in the world can stop them."

I drink from the cup in front of me and taste whole milk. I ask if there's any coffee.

"Coffee thins your blood," she says. She is hungover, but her hair is washed. She's wearing a pink t-shirt, lipstick, and jeans. Dark patches hang from her eyes. I ask if she partied last night.

She smiles and shakes her head. "Stephen won 300 dollars at the track. I don't know why I drank. I know I shouldn't, but we were having such a good time. It didn't seem wrong."

She looks down. "He makes me feel good, you know. Lets the sunshine in. Makes me forget about the troubles we've had. You don't have to hate him."

She checks on the muffins and sits back down. She says, "I used to tell myself, if I stopped drinking and swearing, then God would bring your brother back. I thought I could make a bargain, turn back the past. Everyone tries to do that. We all think we could have been better people, and that might have changed things."

She puts her hands on top of mine. "I think you feel that way, too, Jack. I think you're trying to make a bargain with God."

I pull my hands away. Hers aren't a mother's hands anymore. They stopped being a mother's hands when she touched Uncle Bones everywhere he wanted her.

We eat in silence when the muffins are done. The blueberries stain our tongues.

––––––––

I try to nap in the afternoon but can't sleep. When I close my eyes I see faces in the bottom of the river. Uncle Bones, naked, on the living room couch. Our house sinking slowly in an ocean of brown water. We are almost entirely water, Nathanial said once. If we bleed to death, our water drains out of us. Our water becomes free.

When we were kids, Nathanial brought me the change from his pockets. Every night, he came to my room and turned his jeans inside out looking for nickels, dimes, and quarters. When I go down to the river, I'm not trying to make a wish. I'm not trying to buy my dead brother passage to the other side. I'm trying to drown him.

One thing about Nathanial. He could do all those drugs, but he couldn't swim. It terrified him—his head slipping underneath dark water; the currents pulling him down by the ankles; knowing that as soon as he tried to breathe, that was it.

At twenty years and five and a half days old, I've lived as long as Nathanial ever did. I can outlast him. But part of me wishes I'd been there in the attic, struggling to breathe. We could have faced it together as brothers, the same blood in our veins, unshaken as the spiked heroin inched toward our hearts like a lit fuse.

———

The night my brother died, I was down by the river with my old girl-friend, trying to get her to touch me between my legs. A girl from high school. I can't even remember what she looks like. She let me slip my hands up her shirt and under her bra. That was important at the time. We sat on the levee with our shoes dangling over the water, our tongues pressed together.

As I guided her hand toward my zipper, Nathanial sat in the at-tic, tightening a rubber hose around his arm.

When she undid my pants and held me with pink hands, I must have looked like Uncle Bones. Head back, eyes closed, mouth open. Ready to explode.

———

I stand beneath the trapdoor that leads to the attic. The opening is the only space on the ceiling not covered by paper.

This is how it happens if I choose to go into the attic. I will pull down the trapdoor, grasp the wooden rungs, and hoist myself into the hot, stale room. Dust and insulation will float past my face like air-bag powder after a head-on collision. Nathanial is there, fuzzy in the darkness. He is sitting and watching. I step forward, but the

130

closer I get, the more he disappears. An empty rocking chair, ropes dangling from the arms.

My nose will be convinced that the musty smell is blood, brother's blood. I'll crawl on my knees, feeling for wetness along the rough, dry plywood. When I make the far side of the attic, I'll clench my fists and beat the floor. The skin on my knuckles will break. My face will fall, and I'll bleed and cry into the ceiling above my bed the way Nathanial wanted me to all along. I'll leak blood and tears. The water will drain out until there's nothing left.

I asked him once, what was so important? Why do these things to yourself?

He asked if I looked forward to each day. I said, sure. Some days more than others.

He said that he didn't look forward to any days. It was like watching a movie. He could never sit all the way through a film because he knew it would end, and then the movie would be over. It made him feel like crying. How could you enjoy something that you knew was going to end? He said movies should go on forever. The soundtrack should keep playing. The credits should never roll. The cameras should continue filming until the end of time.

Nighttime comes. I check the clock. It's over, now. I've lived an entire day longer than Nathanial lived. There's no reason for me to climb into the attic. He won't be up there much longer. I wasn't around when he died, but he watched me outlive him. He always had to go first, sniff out danger. But he doesn't know what it's like to be twenty years and six days old. No more leading the way. He's got to trust that Little Jack can take care of himself.

I stand on my bed and pull the pins out of the papers. Every fourth pin releases a white sheet that teeters and floats to the floor. No water spots on the back, clean.

Light flashes through the window. I open the glass so the cool

March wind can carry the papers into the sky or tuck them under the bed. Lightning stitches through blackness. Thunder shakes the branches. Uncle Bones is wrong. It is going to rain.

Underneath me, I can hear people arguing. It's my mom and Uncle Bones. Their voices come up through the floor. My mom's voice is louder, angry. I sit on the bed and close my eyes. The rain starts to fall, softly at first, but then harder, and harder still, as if the world is relearning how to clean itself. The papers blow across the floor. They brush against my feet, wrap around the legs of the bed.

Time passes; I don't know how much. Downstairs grows quiet. My mom and Uncle Bones have stopped fighting. Maybe they have made up. She could have sent him away. Or maybe they are having sex. It doesn't matter. I don't need to live here anymore.

I move to the window and look out at the lawn. It is raining hard enough to stir the coins on the bottom of the river. Hard enough to wash the mud off the tops of graves.

I lean out the window and listen. My hair is soaked. My face is wet. Uncle Bones is out in the yard, now, drunk. He staggers in the rain, shirtless. Dark jeans plastered against his legs, t-shirt crushed in his fist. He is trying to face his fears—challenging the night, catching the storm in his outstretched hands. When the thunder settles, I can hear him yelling. He wants to make sure there are no dead people in the yard, wants them to stop hiding from him. He kneels in the mud, raises both arms.

Go and get him, Nathanial. Do something for me.

Go get Uncle Bones.

SNOW GEESE

The man at the grocery store says snow geese are setting the sky on fire. They migrate north along the bend of the Missouri River, stopping a mile or so east of the Loess Hills to form a super flock— a place they consider halfway home. Thirty thousand birds sitting in a harvested field. Sixty thousand wings corralled by the folds of the only blown together hills in North America.

Marcus, like the geese, is also halfway home. Two homes, two destinations. The grocery store where he bags the man's green vegetables and canned soup is located two miles north of his father's house, and two and a half miles southeast of his mother's townhome. The difference between him and the geese, of course, is that he travels alone. Ever since he was a child, he's spent Saturday through Monday with his father, Tuesday through Friday with his mother. Two families, two bedrooms.

"Go on highway M towards Stanberry, not far," the man at the store says. "You won't have to look hard. More often geese find you." Marcus would like to see that: thousands of snow geese in the wind, blowing together like feathers from a torn pillow. He promises the man he will check it out.

Later that night, Marcus wakes in his father's recliner to the sound of the back door opening, the light of the kitchen flickering on. He hears the buzz of the fridge compressor, and the tinkle of ice filling a glass. His father stands in the entryway between kitchen and living room; his oversized body nearly eclipses the opening, giant flannel shirt split and un-tucked. "You here tonight?" he asks.

"Mom's out."

Marcus' dad eases his large frame onto the couch. "Royals looking hard at that released Mets prospect," he says. He flicks on the news, cracks a two liter of Mountain Dew, and thumbs open a large bag of beef jerky. He's been eating the same thing for months. The guys at the plant claimed you could lose weight if you ate jerky as a snack instead of potato chips. Marcus can picture his dad, like a looped video, lifting strips of meat to his lips, chewing and chewing, then washing it away with yellow fizz. Countless signs for fast food and oncoming headlights swim across the semi-truck windshield. One hand on the wheel, one hand reaching for more. This is his father's life. Day trips to Saint Louis, long trips to Nashville. Beef jerky and Diet Mountain Dew.

When Marcus was a kid, his dad let him check the oil and tire pressure at rest stops. He is old enough now to drive a shift while the other man sleeps in the cab, but the insurance laws changed, and his dad says driving truck is no future to want. There's more to life than the work you do.

"You're chewing that stuff like bubble gum," Marcus says.

His dad doesn't take his eyes off the television. He gestures to the two empty bottles of Bud Light on the coffee table. "Don't make drinking my beer a habit."

That is the last thing they say to each other. The news plays on the television, then *Letterman*, then *SportsCenter*. Marcus dozes in the recliner, and eventually stumbles toward his bedroom. His dad is fast asleep on the sofa. The heat comes in heavy through the floor vents of Marcus' room. He sprawls shirtless across the bed.

A long time ago Marcus recognized that his father rarely sleeps in the bedroom when he is home. They never owned a crib or toddler bed. Little Marcus slept curled between his dad and a body pillow so he wouldn't roll off the mattress. After that, a cot next to his dad's bed. In second grade, Marcus demanded his own room, but his dad still made a habit of falling asleep near him. Marcus never thought it strange. He would be playing with Hot Wheels in

134

the living room or doing his homework or talking on the phone, and he would turn to find his father fast asleep on the couch or in the recliner. His dad was always tired, he decided, or, maybe, his dad simply had a hard time sleeping in an empty house.

At 2:30 AM, a text message from Brittni wakes Marcus. He goes downstairs and lets her in. She isn't wearing anything under her sweatshirt and sweatpants. In his bedroom, she guides his hands underneath her clothes, but she doesn't allow him to take anything off. She is too worried his father will open the door without knocking. Marcus knows his dad will never wake up. Even if he does, it won't matter. He won't care.

"I'm going to be tired tomorrow," Brittni says. "I can't stay much longer."

He shrugs. "Drink lots of coffee."

She kisses him on the wrist. "I'm trying very hard not to have sex with you," she says.

She doesn't mean it, but he told her to say it. If they aren't going to have sex, she should always pretend like she wants to.

Here's a secret Marcus doesn't know: When she gets home later that night she'll stand naked in front of her bedroom mirror—one hand over her breasts, the other between her legs. This is what it will feel like, she'll think. She spreads out on the bed and tries to imagine Marcus without his shirt, his thin muscles tight under skin; the outside of Marcus' legs against the inside of her thighs; his breathing in her ear. "It's okay," he tells her. "This is what we've always wanted." Instead, all she can picture is the face of a man named Richard Young, her father's best friend—handsome and strong and thirty-three years old. She imagines Richard Young tapping on her door in the middle of the night, and when she answers, sweeping her into his powerful arms and kissing her with his peppermint mouth. She thinks of Richard Young under the covers, the scratch of his whiskers, his hands searching for her breasts. He's so warm, and she wants to drown in his warmth, choke on it. Don't be afraid, Richard, she whispers. Don't ever stop touching me.

"Marcus, if you get your own place next year, I can spend the night," she says.

"Either that, or we could move away," says Marcus. "Go somewhere nobody recognizes us."

"Don't say things like that," she says. "I turned down three schools to stay here."

He is sleepy. He doesn't feel like talking. "That's fine. Whatever you think is fine."

———

The next day at school, Marcus sleeps through study hall. The senior boys can sit at the back table and do as they please. The teacher on duty, Richard Young, is also the assistant football coach. He and Brittni's father are best friends. He places his hand on Marcus' shoulder when the period ends. The rest of the students have already filed toward their lockers. "Hey man," he says. "It's eighth hour."

Marcus rubs his eyes. He has been dreaming about snow geese, the way a bird can float in the wind, high above the clouds. Could a bird get lost? He wants to drive north of town over the weekend, see if he can find them.

"Coach," he says, "you heard about these geese that showed up all of a sudden?"

"I pass snows everyday on the way to school. A hundred million of them," says Richard Young. "If they were in season, I'd bag a couple."

"They look like fire in the sky, right?"

"I don't know about that. If I shot at them, that might look like fire. Two shots, I'd have a limit."

Richard Young holds up his hands and pretends to shoot a shotgun.

"One. Two," he says. "Dead sky rats."

———

The eighteen-year-old version of Marcus' mother, the same age he is now, decided she loved Marcus' dad so much that two skipped birth control pills weren't a reason for panic. If they didn't have sex during ovulation, she couldn't get pregnant. But that wasn't true. Her next period never came. She told Marcus' dad she was terribly ill, something was truly wrong, but she wasn't pregnant. He begged her not to move out, but she couldn't hide her growing stomach, and she didn't know how to tell him that even though she loved him, she could never marry a guy who would drive a semi-truck until his heart wore out—a guy who would continue to grow and soften as he aged until his body simply gave up on itself.

After Marcus was born, she realized she could not raise a child alone. The paychecks were spent before they were made, her stepmom and dad were separating, and her friends all had full-time jobs of their own. She sent a photograph in the mail. "This is your son. I'm sorry," it said. That was the bad time, when she was afraid of Marcus' dad. His pickup truck would show up during the middle of the night, and he would sit there in her driveway with the engine idling. She ventured out finally, wearing a blanket over her nightgown, and asked him why he wouldn't leave her alone. She thought he would scream, threaten to kill her. Instead, he said in a soft voice, "I just want to see him." She brought the sleeping baby out, and he held the child on his belly. Both arms rested against the steering wheel like a makeshift cradle. His thick fingers moved gently against the soles of his son's tiny feet, discovering for the first time something unbelievably small and breakable in his hands. Everything that mattered, she realized in a moment of sharp clarity, was in his hands.

"If he wakes up," he said, "he won't know who I am."

"He likes it if you rub his back," she said, suddenly overwhelmed by the fact that Marcus' dad was stronger than her. She could barely close the passenger door before her eyes filled. If he wanted to, he could take the baby away, and she could do nothing to stop him. Each step from the truck seemed to place an incredible distance between herself and her child. By the time she made it inside, she crumpled against the entryway like a discarded winter jacket, too tired to sleep, too tired to stay awake, too tired to think of herself as anything more than a mother who gave her baby away.

When the sun came up, she heard a knock. Marcus' dad handed the baby back and asked to use the bathroom. He looked different, grateful; he didn't look angry.

This became a regular occurrence. The truck would pull up in the middle of the night, and she'd bring the kid out. After a while, she learned to sleep better when her son was out in the driveway, sleeping in the cab of his father's truck.

———

After school, Marcus pulls into his mom's driveway. His mother is sitting on the patio, smoking a cigarette. Boyfriend's car isn't parked on the street.

"Hey handsome," his mother says. "How was school?"

It was fine. It was always fine. She tries to tussle his hair, but he pulls away.

"So you stayed at your dad's last night," she says. It isn't a question. "You need to let me know when you do that."

"Okay."

"We're having company for dinner," she says. She means Boyfriend is coming over. "I need you to peel potatoes."

"I'm eating at Brittni's."

"I don't think so."

"Well, they're planning on me."

"Fine," she says. "Do whatever you want."

She takes a long drag and holds the smoke in her lungs. Lately, she's been buying cigarettes two packs at a time. Here's another secret Marcus doesn't know: some days his mother wishes he would disappear. She hates the thought. It's not that she doesn't love him. She does, so much. But he is impossible. He reminds her of all the mistakes she made in life.

She looks at him: eighteen years old, burning her face with his eyes. She wishes he were little again. They loved you so much more when they were little, but he's all grown up. They become unstoppable when they grow up.

"It wouldn't kill you to stay here once in a while," she says.

On their first date, Marcus drove Brittni to Kansas City. The sun dipped below the horizon on the trip home. When they entered the Missouri River valley, all Marcus could see were the few pinhole stars above, and the thirty feet or so of interstate brightened by his headlights. He knew to look for deer in the ditch. It was the rut—the time of year when young bucks lost their reservations. They would run blindly toward the scent of a doe. Marcus knew how to spot the reflection of their eyes, the bouncing white tails, but he didn't expect a juvenile buck to come from the left, across two lanes of southbound traffic and the median.

It was a shadow in the road until he hit it. Then it was a deer's body, rolling away from his headlights into the shoulder. The airbags deployed, cracking the windshield. Marcus figured that the loud noise was the impact, but it was actually from his own mouth. Smoke and dust filled the car. He could swear he heard an alarm going off.

"I can't breathe," Brittni said.

"Get out of the car," he said. His voice was shaking. He helped her open the door. The air bag had jammed her fingers, burned the skin on her bare knees.

The buck was dead when Marcus checked it. One of its stubby antlers had been knocked off. Its eyes were still open. He nudged the body with his foot. "I didn't mean to hurt you," he said to the deer.

Brittni was hugging herself, and she pressed against him when he offered his coat. He could feel her slender arms reach beneath his sleeves and wrap around his back. The next thing he knew she was kissing him with an open mouth—their first kiss—standing in the interstate shoulder between the totaled car and fallen deer. His eyes were closed, but he could feel the wind from the cars flying by in the night. He could sense the passing headlights flash upon his face.

———

Clearly, one of the innate talents of a snow goose is flying in loops around hundreds of friends and family without colliding. Long ago, they abandoned the majestic V of their Canadian cousins in favor of a disjointed, horizon-to-horizon stretching U. Upon reaching or leaving a destination, snow geese tend to swirl around like snowflakes in a blizzard. Each year the birds follow the Central Flyway migration route, straddling the eastern edge of the Great Plains from the warmth of Mexico in the winter to the Artic breeding grounds in the summer. Seeing them in an open field is often a sign that cold is coming to an end, and spring is four or five weeks away. In a year or two, Marcus will see the geese as a reminder of time continuing forward, the seasons' continual change.

Like all geese, snows mate for life, and the mother and father guard the chicks like angry bulls until they see their young leave the ground for the first time. Unlike smaller birds, a young goose can immediately swim, but takes nearly two months to learn how to catch the air under its wings. A goose will stay with its family for several years before taking a mate, and, sometimes, the same geese will migrate together for the rest of their lives. North to south, south to north, never parting.

Marcus will one day find himself hiking in the Loess Hills of northwest Missouri, unknowingly navigating the same ripples of earth that guide the snow geese. At the top of the trail crest, he will turn in a slow circle, taking a panorama of the surrounding land: the muddy river to the west, the soft line of hills running north and south, the flatness of his home to the east. He'll kill his iPod's volume and wipe his face, thinking all the while about wind and its ability to shape things: the clouds; the sediment, stripped from farm soil; the hills themselves, built literally from dust; the geese, routed by the breeze; he, Brittni, his mom and dad. Everything blown together. Everything blown apart.

"Here comes trouble," Richard Young says when Marcus walks into the living room. He is sitting on the couch next to Brittni. Brittni's father is sitting in his armchair, drinking a gin and tonic.

"Coach," says Marcus.

"Hey kid. How's your mom doing?" says Brittni's father. He is wearing prescription sunglasses and chewing a straw. After three drinks, autopilot takes over.

"She's fine. Brittni and I were going to get a burger if that's okay. Can I pick you guys up one?"

Richard Young looks at Brittni. "You could stick around. We're going to watch a movie."

"Let 'em go have fun, Rich," says Brittni's father.

Marcus is in a hurry. He drives Brittni to the dead end of Stevenson Park. She holds his hand as he drives. He speeds, and he never speeds, not since he hit the deer. After they park, he removes her shirt, and then her bra. Several minutes later they share the passenger seat, and he reaches his hand down the front of her jeans. He feels her pressing against him, the soft tangle of hair beneath her underwear. She pulls away when he finds what he's searching for.

"What's wrong?"

"It doesn't feel good," she says.

He sits back in his own seat. "Jesus, Brittni. I know you won't sleep with me, but now you don't want to do anything."

"Just lean back," she says. "I'll make you feel good."

"Are you sure?"

"Of course."

She closes her eyes. She doesn't mind doing the things that he likes, but lately it doesn't feel the same. Lately, she counts the seconds in her head until he shudders and tells her how much he loves her and how he is going to marry her one day and they are going to make love on their wedding night with the lights on. She used to think they were progressing toward something bright, something important, but now it seems like she is lying to him with her lips when she kisses him. His skin feels like nothing.

There's a reason why Brittni only pictures Richard Young when she touches herself in the middle of the night. The reason, of course, waits for Marcus' headlights to pull away from Brittni's driveway before sneaking down the darkened hall. She cannot see his face when he opens the door, but she senses him standing next to her bed, the smell of him, his peppermint breathing. His strong hands rub her back, underneath her shirt. They feel like love, but Richard Young doesn't love her. She can see the outline of his tall frame in the dark.

They never make love. Not yet. That's off limits. But Richard is there two nights a week, touching her body, feeling her delicate curves and bends. Some nights, they kiss for hours. They both know it won't be long before he whispers in her ear that he must have her, just once, just for a little bit. The time when a spade becomes a spade, and inappropriate becomes invasion. If he is, in fact, irredeemable, he won't turn back. He'll jump the rest of the way in.

It hadn't started out as much. Get me a glass of orange juice, and I will give you a kiss on the cheek, she had said. Innocent. It seemed long ago, when he had turned his lips against hers in the kitchen. "I'm sorry," he said, backing away with her taste in his mouth, but she said she wasn't sorry. She said thank you. He watched her ass as she walked away; so young, so unmistakably young, but unmistakably sexual. It was her, he realized. She must have kissed him; her grip had crushed his sleeve. Days later, he spied her coming out of the bathroom wearing only a towel, hair a wet mess. He couldn't stop thinking about her. Never in his life had he wanted anything so badly. How soft were the palms of her hands? How did she smell beneath her clothing? What cut of underwear fit her best?

The words—I'm having an affair with my best friend's daughter—don't sound real. She's beautiful in the way that only the untouchable can be beautiful. She looks like a woman, but she's something in between. Not woman. Not child. All day he tells himself that if he ends it now, he can still escape, but when he sees her, thoughts stop. The body takes over.

He remembers the night when he crossed the line. Brittni's father had left to refill their drinks, and Brittni walked into the living room wearing a long t-shirt over a flash of yellow panties. She asked who was winning the football game and sat on his knee. Maybe she was just teasing, but he couldn't take it. He pulled her into his lap. She took a sharp breath, but didn't resist. What happened next was instinct. No man could think it wrong. Richard Young was seventeen again, and he was sitting in the dark of his basement bedroom with his high school girlfriend draped all over him. His hands were on her breasts, in her hair, down her underwear. He was breathing heavily, and all that mattered was the body in front of him. It was like guzzling water when you were only seconds earlier dying of thirst. He couldn't control himself. She was moving her hips against him, and he drank her in as fast as he could.

But it didn't last long. Maybe ten seconds, and then Brittni had him by the wrists. "You need to stop," she said. "He's coming back." And those three words sobered him. What had he done? For the rest of his days, he would have to live with the fact that he had felt the warmth between the legs of his best friend's daughter; he had fondled her breasts and pressed his erection against her. Names were given to men who act like that: monster, deviant, molester.

The night dragged unbearably on. He sat cross-legged, still rock hard. Meeting her father's eyes was unthinkable. He doesn't remember what they talked about, something stupid like 401(k)s, or if they talked at all. He counted the seconds until the father's head drooped against the back of the easy chair. Richard tried to think of a way to explain. Had he forced himself on her? Was she angry enough to rat him out? Had she liked it? How far could they possibly have gone? Would she have let him slide off her panties? If he asked her, would she close her eyes and mound together the cups of her bra? Women he had dated in their thirties had whisper lines on their legs; their breasts hung like weights from their chests. They had experience, sure, but they could never make him do something completely irrational like he did when he followed Brittni down the hall to her bedroom.

She embraced him when he tapped on her door, pulled him out of the hallway lights into the bedroom's darkness. He felt her hand on the front of his jeans, her tongue in his mouth.

———

"Dad," says Marcus. "Do they need any help at the plant? I was thinking about applying after graduation."

His dad looks away from the television. "Nah, you ain't want to work there."

"It might be a good idea. I could chip in on the mortgage. We could save some cash. Maybe even buy our own rig."

His dad opens another bag of beef jerky and presses a strip into his mouth. He chews it slowly before answering. "You drank a six-pack of beer last night," he says. "I told you not to do that."

"You said I could have one when I'm over here."

"One. Not a six-pack."

Marcus tries to laugh. "All right, sorry. I won't drink a six-pack when I'm over here. Relax."

"Know what your mom would do if she learned you were over here drinking? She'd take me to court. I'd never see you again."

"What are you getting pissed for? I said I was sorry."

His dad takes another hunk of jerky. He looks away when he realizes Marcus is crying. The tone of his voice changes, "I'm not mad, son. We just need to be smarter about things. That's all."

Marcus won't look at him.

"Listen, I'll talk to Ed. It's probably overnight help he needs. It's hard work, but pretty steady. Don't get excited."

———

Years ago, Marcus pointed his father to a single white bird floating in one of the not-yet-frozen ponds you see huddled along Interstate 29 between Kansas City and Omaha. It was the dead of win-

ter, and Marcus cupped his hands around a gas station hot chocolate. He asked if wild swans existed in this part of the country. His
father took his eyes off the road for a moment and shook his head.

"Not a swan," he said. "Too small."

The semi-truck shuddered and rumbled as his father shifted
gears; the white puff of bird dwindled in the side mirror.

"Why would she go swimming by herself?" Marcus said. "I
thought birds liked to be around other birds."

"Maybe the others forgot about it. They're probably down in
the Bahamas soaking up the sunshine."

Marcus wedged the cup between his knees and pressed his
cold hands against the heater vent. "How come they don't freeze
to death in that water?" he said.

"They're built for the cold. Always wearing a nice feather coat."

"Are feathers waterproof?"

"Absolutely."

Marcus touched the frosted window, leaving a handprint in the
ice. He looked out over the empty farm fields, the endless stretch
of highway.

"Dad, I don't think people are built for the cold," he said. "I'm
not."

———

Three days later, Brittni's parents are gone. Richard Young is on his
feet in Brittni's bedroom. His pants are undone, and his arms are
raised as if trying to explain. Marcus isn't listening. He is trying to
hit the coach in the face. He is calling the coach names and saying how he wants to kill him. He doesn't stop until the coach's fist
strikes his jaw. He falls backwards; warmth radiates across his face.

"I'm sorry, Marcus," Richard Young says. "I know it's wrong.
Come on, man, we're friends."

Brittni is out of the bed. She is pulling Marcus into the hall,
shutting the bedroom door on Richard Young who has started to
cry—big, gasping, exaggerated sobs.

"I can't breathe," she says. Her eyes are dry.

"The son of a bitch. He forced you."

"No," she says. "He didn't. It's me. There's something wrong with me."

"It can't be you."

She takes his hands. "I don't understand me," she says.

He wants to look her in the face but cannot raise his eyes from the floor. He hears her asking him, pleading him never to tell. "Promise me, Marcus" she keeps saying. He can sense her squeezing his hands, but it feels like he's standing alone in the hallway.

He thinks back to the car accident, their first kiss, the juvenile buck rolling into the ditch. He pictures them hugging in the glow of headlights. He had been shaking. It wasn't from the sensation of her lips on his. He had been thinking about the other things that might have happened when the deer stepped in front of the car: fishtailing out of control down the steep ditch, getting rear-ended by a semi-truck, the deer's legs coming through the windshield at 75 miles an hour. Those things would have killed him. Either that or he might have regained consciousness to find Brittni sitting beside him, not breathing for real this time.

He is putting his arms around her; she's breaking down. He is burying his face into her hair, listening to her say she's sorry.

———

Marcus drives to his father's house, but the door is locked. His father is working overnight tonight, hauling freight to Albuquerque. Marcus twists the knob, but nothing happens. The deadbolt is fixed. He tries the back, but it is locked as well. He contemplates throwing a rock through the window, threading his hand through the shards. Instead, he kicks at the door. "Goddamn you," he says.

He doesn't knock on his mother's door, just pushes his way inside. It is after midnight. Boyfriend is there, eating Doritos and watching television. His mother's head rests on a pillow placed between his knees.

"Why don't you go to bed," she tells Boyfriend. "I'll be up in a minute."

146

Marcus heads downstairs toward his bedroom.

"Sit down," she says. "I want to talk to you."

He sits on the couch.

"Your father called this morning."

Marcus doesn't say anything.

"He says that he saved enough money for you to get an apartment this summer. A place all to yourself. You don't have to tell anybody if you're coming or going. You don't have to sneak around. You can invite Brittni over any time you want."

"We're not together anymore."

His mother pauses. "I didn't know that."

"Don't worry about it."

"Your dad says you need to take over the lease after the summer. If you want to go to college, he thinks you'll qualify for student loans. If you want to get a full-time job, you shouldn't have any trouble paying rent. You can stay here, too, if you want. You know that, don't you?"

"What if I don't want to live here anymore?"

"That's up to you, I suppose."

Marcus doesn't talk for a long time. Then he says, "Mom, have you ever been to Duluth, Minnesota?"

"No."

"Dad took me there once. There are these hills that go down to Lake Superior, the steepest hills in the world. In the winter, the harbor ices over, and the roads get slick. Anyway, Dad said that if you live at the bottom of the hills, you can watch cars try to drive down. Some of them make it fine, but on the worst days everybody without snow tires slides down the hill. Sometimes they fishtail into people's yards. Sometimes they hop the curbs or smack into light poles. It's unbelievable."

Marcus doesn't say so, but that's where he thinks he belongs, next to real hills, not just blown together mounds of sediment. Someplace where people watch each other go spinning out of control. They stand and scream at the people who crash. What the hell were you thinking, they say. You dumb shit. What did you think was going to happen? Why did you leave your house in the first place?

147

His mom stares at him. She takes his hand. Her eyes are worn out, lost. She wishes she could fold him into her arms and tell him that everything will be okay, but she doesn't say anything. She can't.

———

The next day Marcus drives north of town, desperately trying to find the snow geese, but they are nowhere, and at the same time, they are everywhere. It's snowing in northwest Missouri, big fat flakes, and Marcus imagines for a moment that he can hear them, the geese, beating their wings and trumpeting to the sky. He wishes he could be with them, heading north, even for a single moment, but there are no birds in the air, only the flurries and miles upon miles of field and monotony.

He drives through the gravel roads, searching for some sign of movement in the soft fog where clouds and horizon meet. "Where are you?" he asks out loud.

The roof of his car, the side mirrors, and even the hood are slowly being turned to snow. Soon, like each passing farmhouse, his car will be blanketed in white.

THE FISH ON THE LAKE'S FLOOR

The reservoir lake stretches from the marsh delta of the Central Plains River, eight miles long and one mile wide, to the natural dam the Army Corps of Engineers erected with bulldozers in 1973. *Holding the lake in place*, the locals of Jester say. *Earth and rocks that keep us safe*. Five days a week, the head officer of the Corps of Engineers walks along the foot of the dam, looking for signs of weakness. At night, he dreams about the lake coming loose, a wall of water two stories high, water settling knee-deep in the state capitol streets. If the dam were to fail, he would feel responsible, even though it was not his idea to plug the river so close to urban real estate, not his idea to build middle-class houses in the river valley. Part of him would drown alongside the residents below; part of him would wash away. *People will die if the dam breaks*, the Jester locals say, *lots and lots of people will die under all that water. But we live on the high ground where the lake can't get us.*

A thirty-foot-wide concrete conduit runs underneath the dam and spills out the southern half of the Central Plains River. At 8:30 AM, the head officer performs his daily inspection. He drops to his knees next to the spillway tube, presses his hands in the dirt, feels for erosion. If the ground is a little soft, his heart beats faster; he blinks his eyes more than usual. Today he gives thanks for hard ground beneath his fingers.

Lower on the hill, seventeen-year-old Lyle Gibson snaps digital pictures of the spillway's violent water. To Lyle, the spillway is like a giant faucet. When the faucet is on, it makes a river; off, the river dries up. In the aquatic control tower above him, the Corps of Engineers dictates the flow—a gentle bubbling in drought, frothy rapids during stationary pond, and a screaming water serpent that white-sprays and writhes up the barrier-walls when the reservoir reaches capacity. Lyle wishes they would always leave the gates wide open. He likes it best when water is whitest.

Locals claim over a dozen suicides have taken place at the spillway. *It's like instant death,* they say, *like jumping into a volcano.* Last summer, a man in his sixties from a different state drove a rental car up the access road. He climbed over the guardrail and waved to the fishermen snagging catfish and bass. Then he dove face first into the hurricane of white water. Lyle Gibson had been so shocked he could not raise his camera to document the event, but he remembers the outline of the man falling, and then nothing-ness, like a leaf floating in front of a pressure hose. Several miles downstream, the body bobbed to the surface, as bloated and wa-terlogged as if it had spent a fortnight underwater. "There's only a handful of people that ever see a thing like that," Lyle tells anyone who will listen. "Capturing a dude's last moment. That's a picture worth a thousand words."

When he climbs the rocks to the top of the dam, Lyle can see the bubble of Jester's water tower rising from the trees. He can see the bridge, referred to by locals as the Mile, crossing the skinny part of the reservoir, connecting the town of Jester to the west-bound interstate. To the north and east, dense forest blocks the town from the rest of the state. Perhaps he sees the shape of Crazy Ken who walks across the Mile four times a day, shirtless, even in winter. Crazy Ken says his walking keeps the crocodile-faced aliens from leveling the town with anti-matter guns. He wears a muff hat with earflaps, lined with tinfoil to protect from brain-reading devices, and claims he cannot feel the cold after being struck by secondary lightning in 1989. In Julys, he shaves his long hair and donates the strands to Locks of Love.

Below Lyle Gibson's parked Chevy Cavalier, on the lake side of the dam, pontoons and speedboats anchor in Cerveza Cove. *Kids shouldn't look down there in summer*, the locals say. *They'll get an education they don't need.* Cerveza Cove is famous for margarita drinking contests, empty booze bottles in the water, and twenty dollars for every bikini top thrown in the air. *That cove is Hispanic property. Spanish Harlem, Little Mexico*, locals say to each other at Jimmy's Gas Station. *We should write the city council, get it shut down for good.*

The people of Jester use the lake for shore fishing, mostly. In-town boats are stored behind garages on yellow grass, their engines covered with garbage sacks. On sunny days, tourists flock to the main basin dragging jet-skis and big-horsepower watercraft behind SUV's. Their children ride on inner-tubes hooked to speeding boats. They glide across the glass surface, bounce in the chop, and cry in SpongeBob lifejackets when their tube flips and they are left alone in deep water. The parents circle back, holding up an orange flag. They don't think, like Dave Hertz does, about the average of nine people who drown on the lake every year. They don't think another boat will cut across their wake and catch a child with its prop, but these things happen.

When Dave Hertz's four-year-old nephew fell out of a fishing boat, Dave dove, again and again, opening his eyes and thrashing like a blind man in a wall-less room. He dove until his lungs burned and his eyes turned red. When he could not dive anymore, he treaded water by the boat, yelling his nephew's name, his bladder emptying down his leg.

Late at night, while Dave watches the light from his television flicker on the ceiling tiles, Jester parents in warm bedrooms spin ghost stories into their children's ears. The most commonly told is the legend of twin boys who hold hands and walk across the water's surface in moonlight. The two boys, the Hoffman twins, were drowned by their mother on the night before the lake iced over in December—*donning its winter skin over a madwoman's evils*, the parents say, *lithium possessed her like a witch's spell. It guided her hands as she held her children under the hardening water.* She admitted to the crime, but the bodies were never found. Some say their small forms sank in the cold; the currents pulled them into a submarine grave. Others think they rise up in the middle of the night and walk, blind in the darkness, weeping and feeling for a way out of the water. Crazy Ken says folks who believe in the Hoffman Twins are loony fuckers.

Crazy Ken knows that, underneath eighty feet of water, paddlefish and one-hundred-year-old sturgeon scull like quiet nightmares. He knows that massive flathead catfish, larger than Labradors, snuffle along the bottom, feeling their way over sunken boats, trash, and bodies that have not yet risen to the surface. On weekdays, Crazy Ken argues with Arnold Thompson, who works at Jimmy's Gas Station, about whether the deep fish have ever been caught. Arnold Thompson swears his brother-in-law hooked a sturgeon once, but cut the line when he saw the fish's bearded face. "He thought he had caught a water demon," Arnold Thompson says, "a thing from the Cretaceous. Fish-a-saurus."

At midnight, Lyle Gibson walks along the Mile bridge, digital video camera in hand. Swollen tributaries from weeks of northern rain have flooded the lake. Forty feet below, chocolate waves lap the abutments. Holding himself steady with one skinny arm, Lyle leans over the guardrail and films the moving water. He thinks about people who have thrown themselves from this bridge—tumbling end over end toward the water. He wonders what the thrill was like, the sensation of body in flight, the knockout punch at the end. Slipping out of his backpack, he rummages out and lowers a bight of rope, letting it unravel to full length before reeling it in. He feels the end of the rope for wetness, then ties it off on the guardrail. Double knot on top of double knot. He fastens his video camera to the other end, turns the lens on his face.

"My name is Lyle Joshua Gibson, and I am about to jump off the Mile bridge. If I do not survive this experiment, my dying wish is to be cremated into ashes and mixed with birdseed. Then, when I am all bird food, I want to be fed to the baby osprey in the Cottonwood rookery, so my remains can be shit all over the miserable lake that killed me."

He dangles the video camera over the edge and lets it drop. The camera spins, lens first, toward water. The rope whizzes through his fingers, not quite at falling speed but close enough, until it shudders at full length. He starts to pull in the rope, but stops when the back of his neck chills—the feeling he gets when he realizes someone is watching.

"The hell do you think you're doing?" says Crazy Ken, shirtless, from behind.

"Just something for school," Lyle says. His hands move quicker on the line. "It's a documentary."

"What about?"

"The bridge."

"You got to be careful up here, boy. This isn't a place for messing around. Long way down to that water."

The camera pulls within reach. Lyle unhooks it. He runs his hands over the buttons, checking for damage. "Would you mind if I ask you some questions?" he says. "Do you know anything about this bridge?"

"30 Gypsy Bridge. I know a thing or two, I suppose," Crazy Ken says. He points down the highway. "Keep your camera trained there, hear? You can pick up my voice, but my face ain't right for no movies. Hear me?"

Lyle does as he is told. He asks, "Why did you call it 30 Gypsy Bridge?"

"Because that's its name, sure. Built 27 years ago by the wicked Corps of Engineers. President Tricky Dick signed off on the plans himself. Thirty concrete legs on the bridge. Buried inside each one is a dead gypsy, drowned in cement by the Corps of Engineers with a congressman watching."

"Have you ever seen anyone jump off the bridge?"

"One time," says Crazy Ken. "A terrible thing jumping from this high. Water becomes hard like ice. Spics can survive it, cliff-divers, they slip in the water like a knife between ribs, but the drunks that try it here. Chalk outlines. If the water is too low it pulls your arms and legs off. The fellow I saw—drunk, drunk—he and his friends below in the boat. The lake was up, way up, and this drunk landed feet first. A big splash and those guys in the boat cheer. The drunk, he comes up screaming, 'My balls! My balls! My balls went inside of me!' And I can't help it, I start busting my guts, see, because this guy, he thinks he's being a man jumping off the bridge, but really the lake turned him into a lady."

Crazy Ken laughs, a gurgling sound. Lyle takes a step back, but keeps filming the road, never taking his eyes off the bearded man's face. "One of these days I'll try it myself," Crazy Ken says. "Dive so deep that my belly will scrape bottom mud and I'll give my regards to the skeletons of them who didn't make it. But that will be a long time from now, and no one will miss me."

––––––

"Let me tell you a story," says Earnest Speas to Heather Reed in the parked car at Kingfisher Point. He reaches a hand between her thighs; runs a finger on the seam of her jeans. He does it slowly as if circling a penny on a tabletop. She closes her eyes; doesn't feel any pleasure, only pressure. "I was on the beach last weekend, and there was a drunk there with his little girl. This drunk was so wasted that he passed out on the sand while the three-year-old girl swam by herself. Finally, some mom pulled the girl out of the water and called the cops. So this big muscleman sheriff, he shows up all pissed off, and he picks up the sleeping drunk by the hair—I mean, he literally grabbed this fucker by the scalp and hauled him to his feet. The sheriff looks the drunk right in the eye and says, 'I need you to identify the body of a little girl who just drowned.'

"Then the drunk starts crying, and he's hitting himself in his own face with his fist. The cop feels bad, so he gets the three-year-old out of the squad car to show that she's still alive, but the drunk is so messed up that he thinks the little girl is dead, even though she's blinking at him and calling him Daddy. He punches himself harder and harder; blood's coming out his nose and one of his eyes. The cop doesn't know what to do, so he cuffs the guy and takes him to jail."

Ernest looks out the windshield. He points to the sloped beach below the parking lot. "All that happened right there." He touches his girlfriend harder, digging his fingers into the denim. He thinks he feels wetness.

"Am I doing this right?" he asks. She nods. He lays his face on her shoulder and thinks he should tell her about the other time— the time when a twelve-year-old boy did actually drown, how all the people on the beach made a human chain and walked arm in arm through the swimming area until someone bumped the sunken body. He wants to tell her about the drowned boy touching his legs underwater, the feel of cold skin against his, and how he didn't want to say anything but couldn't help from squeezing the next people's hands so hard that they began to holler. When the adults pulled out the dripping body, Ernest wanted to close his eyes, but he couldn't look away. They carried the boy onto the beach, taking turns pressing on the chest and breathing into the lungs, but he was long dead.

Ernest lets his hand fall away from Heather Reed's jeans. "I am in love with you," he wants to say. "I think we could spend the rest of our lives together." He wants to mean it, too, but he doesn't. Instead, he asks her to take off her shirt. She pulls her top and sports bra over her head; sets them on the dash. In the dark, her nipples take the shape of starlight's soft reflection on water.

On Friday nights, Dave Hertz walks from his ranch house past Jester Town Square in search of the Lighthouse Bar. When he finds it, he shoulders the heavy door open and stumbles to the barstool, already drunk from pre-drinking. "I saw a bird, today," he tells Emilio the Latino bartender. "A bird that no one has ever seen before. And they're going to name it after me."

Emilio holds up a tattooed hand. He brings Dave a Tom Collins and puts a finger to his lips. "Hertz," he says, "you need to be quiet tonight. I need these tips to make rent."

"You got it, Holmes," says Dave. He sets money on the counter, swishes the cocktail in his mouth before swallowing.

On nights like these, Emilio tries to talk Dave out of buy-ing some company, but he is never able. Emilio reaches into his pocket, pulls out a cell phone, and dials the number of his cousin, who shows up fifteen minutes later and gives Dave oral sex in the back room. She makes him close his eyes when she does it, and refuses intercourse—no matter how much he begs or is willing to pay. Once it is over, he makes her hold him and say how much she enjoyed it, which she does, because he slips a twenty-dollar bill down her shirt and whispers that she is the one. He says he wants to swim in the dark pools of her eyes and drown in the blood of her *corazón*. When she leaves the bar, Emilio puts his head down. He polishes a glass or slides the liquor bottles closer together. He acts as if he has walked in on her taking a shower, as if he has caught her beating a child. Outside, she slides two sticks of peppermint gum into her mouth and chews until the taste disappears.

———

In early September, 8000 pelicans gather on the Central Plains Riv-er delta. They are scared of jet skis and speedboats, so they don't paddle farther south into the reservoir. From the Mile, the huddle of birds looks like a shallow white island. Bird watchers and orni-thologists from the Cottonwood Rookery say that the lake serves as a kind of two-week hotel for resting, preening, and getting fat off fish before the next leg of the south migration. Tourists ask about the pelicans at Jimmy's Gas Station. Arnold Thompson says they are like big geese—noisy and shitting everywhere, scaring off the egrets and herons, fouling up the ecosystem. He doesn't know if any of this is true, but he guesses it is. On his smoke break, he tells the skateboard kids that seagulls are conceived when a peli-can fucks a robin. "The mama robin can never again lay eggs after squeezing out a gull," he says. "It's like giving birth to a 3rd grader." The skateboard kids pay him 75 cents for single cigarettes.

Heather Reed thinks the pure whiteness of a pelican's feathers is a sign of God's love. She fantasizes about catching a baby pelican and bathing it in soapy water until it glows.

Crazy Ken tells people that he only believed in God for fifteen minutes. It was an after-rain sundown. The seagulls were criss-crossing the Mile in a frenzy, their sharp bills snapping up June bugs and mosquitoes. The little birds looked like a flurry of snow-flakes as they weaved back and forth in the light. The silver tips of their wings shined like reflectors, their ringing calls like odes to saltwater. Crazy Ken removed his muff hat and gave thanks. With the gulls swirling around him, he was invincible. He could stand in front of the spillway canal and bear the entire weight of the lake like a reservoir Atlas.

A blast from a passing semi-truck's horn scattered the birds and left Crazy Ken crumpled against the guardrail. He waited for the seagulls to come back, but the sun went down and he stopped believing in God again.

After school, Lyle Gibson works up the courage to ask Heather Reed over to watch his documentary on the Mile. In his parents' basement, they watch the crudely rendered film on his computer. As she takes it in, he wonders if she knows that he made the movie to impress her. When the screen goes black, he cranes his neck to-ward her, his lips softening.

Every winter, after the head officer of the Corps of Engineers posts the "safe depth" sign in the town square, people venture onto the ice. The head officer waits to see geese waddle across first, and when silver coyotes snivel along the edge like ghosts, he knows it is three days of good freeze from solid. In the dead of winter, locals swish patterns through the powder with grumbling snowmobiles. They drive trucks across as if the ice were a smooth valley between the east and west banks. Locals say it is a safe lake, *deep lakes make for thick ice,* but every couple of years the earliest vehicles slip through. It is usually planned—a junker with a jimmy-rigged pedal, guided out by the Corps of Engineers to test the ice.

In the year 2000, seven high school seniors drove their pickups down the Cherry Grove boat ramp and spent the night doing doughnuts and figure eights in the lake's basin. The police report says the heat from the friction weakened the ice, and the trucks went down when a large rift broke open. Early next morning a blizzard moved through the state, dumping seven inches of snow. A thin film of slush and ice closed over the lake's opening like a scar.

That night, at Cherry Grove's shoreline, the head officer of the Corps of Engineers pulled his Silverado alongside an old man in a beat up Oldsmobile. With the windows down, their breath made steam as they stared across the reservoir.

"It's pretty," the head officer said, "After the snow falls, everything seems clean. Like starting over, almost."

The wind blew, spreading the powder across the lake. In the distance, the dam rose like a mountain out of the flat. Light from river valley houses glowed softly above its crest, illuminating the jagged containment rocks and guardrail, fading out into the patchwork of stars. "Mind if I bum a smoke?" asked the head officer. The old man passed him a cigarette and lighter. The head officer thanked him and took a long drag. He stifled a cough; he hadn't smoked in five years, and never a filter-less cigarette.

"I come out here sometimes when things don't make sense," he said. "Been doing it since I was eighteen. Do you believe that?"

"Seems like a good place to come think," the old man said.

"You come out here often?"

"No, I ain't from around here."

"Welcome to town, then," the head officer said. "Glad to have you."

They smoked in silence. The old man stared blankly across the lake, methodically bringing the cigarette to his lips, then dropping his hand to rest on the side mirror. After a couple minutes, he pointed to the lake. He said, "My grandson is out there, under all that."

―――

Heather Reed cries into Lyle Gibson's skinny shoulder. She cries that he can never tell anyone what they have done for as long as he lives. He says it's okay, strokes her hair, and presses his lips to her forehead. "We just kissed," he tells her, "and it was the best thing ever." But she cries and says no. It was not the best thing; it was the worst. Reaching for her coat, she tries to stand, but he holds her down. She cannot go because he loves her. He loves her so much that he would throw himself into the hurricane of spillway water if she drowned, so they could die the exact same way. If she burned to death, he would bathe in gasoline and put a match to his skin. "You're scaring me," she says. He tries for her lips again, but she won't kiss him, only cries harder. They sit side by side on the couch. Her chest inflates and deflates. "My heart is wide open," he says, placing a hand on her shoulder. She stiffens and pulls away.

He calls her a slut. He says it slowly, purposefully. The word soaks through her. She curls back and strikes, grabbing handfuls of his hair and crushing her face into his. Her tongue flits between his lips, and he is happy in the moments before he feels her warm tears on his cheeks.

―――

Dave Hertz looks through binoculars at the 8000 pelicans floating in the distance. "I wonder why they all came here," he tells Emilio. They are sitting in Dave's truck in one of Cottonwood National Park's scenic overlook lots. Dave takes a swig from his flask and passes.

"They're just like the tourists," says Emilio. "Pretty scenery, sunshine, recreation. Every time they come here it's the same. It's their happy place."

"Birds on vacation?"

"Something like that," Emilio says. "They don't see it every day, so it's pretty to them. First couple times I drove the Mile, I was scared to death—big open bridge, three-foot rails. Now it doesn't bother me. I don't notice the lake anymore."

The pelicans paddle through the delta, slurping up fish and preening their chest and back feathers with tremendous hanging bills. Dave tries to count them, but gives up after fifty. He hands over the binoculars. "I've hated this lake for a decade," he says. "But I've never thought, even for a moment, that she wasn't the prettiest thing I've ever seen."

He dips into his coat and pulls out a rectangular box. "Think you could give this to your cousin?"

"What is it?"

"Oh, she mentioned how much she liked pearls the other day. I was passing by a store and saw this on sale. Thought she might like it. Nothing too big."

Emilio opens the box and inspects the necklace. He squeezes the pearls between his index finger and thumb. "It's nice," he says. "No bullshit. How much did you pay?"

"Seven hundred."

"Jesus, Hertz, I can't give this to her. You know that. Buying her presents isn't going to change anything. That's money down the drain."

Dave leans back. He closes his eyes. "I know. I know. Just give it to her, okay?"

A big pelican flaps its wings and takes off from the water, circles the parking lot, then hangs in the air above the truck for several seconds as if caught in perfect stasis with the wind. It pumps its wings, and they watch as it disappears over the tree line.

"Does she ever talk about me?" Dave asks. "Even a little bit?"

Emilio picks the felt box off the dash. He sets it on the seat between them. "She talks about you," he says. He softens his voice. "She says real nice things, Dave."

———

At the end of September, a leak trickling through the dam sends the head officer of the Corps of Engineers into a panic. As soon as he sees bits of sediment in the flow, his hands start to shake and he reaches for his cell phone. He knows that a pencil hole will widen to the size of a baseball bat in an hour, and, an hour after that, the hole will be large enough to stand in. He asks for a geologist, one who knows dams—one who lives and breathes dam architecture; spends weekends reading books about dams for fun. Finally, a woman calls back. She says she is the best available. She speaks calmly; explains that a boil will equalize the pressure, but the head officer will not relax. "Two stories of water," he says into the phone, trying not to scream. "Do you know how many people that will kill?" The geologist assures him it is just a leak. "Dams leak all the time; they just need pressure to stop bleeding."

Ernest Speas, now serving as a co-op intern for the Army Corps of Engineers, drives a Bobcat loaded with sandbags to the site. He and the head officer spend the rest of the day constructing and reinforcing the boil. "The idea is to build a makeshift well," the geologist says, "This forces water on the shore side to flow back in the lake, and creates equilibrium." The hole grows to the size of a fist, then the size of a grapefruit. Ernest packs mud against the sandbags. He is covered in soil and sweat. "Don't think about stopping," the head officer says. "You don't understand how fast this gets ugly."

The boil fills halfway, but no more. Ernest stands on the sandbags, staring down into the makeshift well. "Looks stable to me," he says. "I think you saved the day, boss." The head officer nods but keeps shoveling dirt and rocks around the sandbags. Hours pass. Not knowing what else to do, Ernest continues to help until five o' clock. His shift ends, and he drives the Bobcat back to the shop to punch out. He does not believe the dam could ever fail.

The head officer stays by the boil, feeling the ground for moisture. After an hour of dryness, he lies on his back next to the sandbags. He prays. Overhead, high above the control tower, the last of the 8000 pelicans do their rounds, floating in lazy figure-eights, making sure no birds are left behind. Heather Reed says the last pelicans to leave are guardian angels; they watch over the town and forgive people their wrongdoings. She and Earnest are sleeping together, now, but she makes him pull out when he finishes.

161

She does not know that Lyle Gibson wrapped his documentary in a Ziploc baggie and dropped it in the spillway the day she left his house.

The head officer continues to pray as the setting sun turns the sky pink. Local geese and seagulls honk and chirp at migrating bird-shapes in the distance, hoping for friendly flocks to turn path. Cars go by on the access road. The wind blows. The head officer thinks about the sturgeon and paddlefish resting on the other side of the dam. He wonders, since one hasn't been caught for so long, if they are still alive.

The fish are down there, hiding in deep water. Oblivious to everything above. Even when Crazy Ken decides it is finally time to dive off the Mile, and his shocked body crashes through to the lake's floor, the fish aren't surprised. Not surprised when Crazy Ken opens his eyes, shoots bubbles from his nose, and searches wildly about for the Hoffman twins, Dave Hertz's nephew, and seven high school seniors trapped in sunken pickup trucks. Not surprised when, high above, Lyle Gibson waves his video camera, screams for help, then slumps against the guardrail, realizing he is alone on the bridge.

The fish don't mind. They keep on swimming, as if none of it had ever happened.